Carrie's

Carrie Hatchett, Space Adventurer #5

J.J. GREEN

This novel uses British spellings.

Second Edition.

ISBN: 978-1981874781
ISBN-10: 198187478X

Cover Design by

Illuminated Images & Dark Moon Graphics

ALSO BY J.J. GREEN

STAR MAGE SAGA

SPACE COLONY ONE SERIES

SHADOWS OF THE VOID SERIES

LOST TO TOMORROW

THERE COMES A TIME
A SCIENCE FICTION COLLECTION

DAWN FALCON
A FANTASY COLLECTION

CONTENTS

ACKNOWLEDGMENTS

I'd like to thank members of the Taipei Writers Group for their unfailing support, constructive criticism and endless demands for chocolate.

PROLOGUE

Penny Lopez had no idea what a sprange flocket was, but that didn't matter. Daddy had told her it shouldn't cost more than two pounds fifty and she could spend the change on sweets. She clutched the three pound coins tightly in her fist and skipped to the shops, wondering if she should buy two lollipops and a cheap bar of chocolate or if she should spend all her money on an expensive chocolate bar with caramel and raisins.

The hardware shop was at the end of the row of shops. Penny had to pass the newsagents to get there. She peeked in through the newsagents' window at the sweets display near the till. Her mouth watered. Maybe she would buy four lollipops and save one for her friend, Joe, who lived next door. If she gave him a lollipop, maybe he would agree to play camping in his garden. Penny pushed open the heavy glass door to the hardware shop, setting the bell jangling.

At first, she didn't notice anything different, except that she couldn't see the owner, Mr. Culverstark, who usually said a cheerful hello. Daddy often sent her on errands to the hardware shop. Mr. Culverstark knew her name and always seemed happy to see her.

Penny surveyed the gloomy, cluttered shop, wondering where Mr. Culverstark had gone. Something moved. She turned towards the thing, but it wasn't Mr. Culverstark. It was a big, heavy piece of equipment that she didn't recognise. It was approaching her.

A scrape and a rustle came from another direction. Penny spun around. Mr. Culverstark was fighting with a contraption made of metal and canvas. The thing was wrapping itself around the old man's head. She could see his eyes above the canvas, wide and white.

The three pound coins Penny was carrying clattered to the floor. She screamed.

Mr. Culverstark managed to work his mouth free. "Penny," he gasped. "Run!"

CHAPTER ONE

Carrie Hatchett was sitting at her new desk in her new office without a clue what she was supposed to do. She looked out the window. Next to the road outside the office block, clear as day, was a big sign saying 'Carrie Hatchett Enterprises'. Carrie turned on her computer. Folders relating to the various business dealings and internal concerns of her new company peppered the screen. She sighed.

It had been very nice to discover that she was the owner of a company after returning from an assignment that had sent her back in time. It had been especially nice that it was the company she'd only recently been fired from. Yet she was beginning to wonder if she was really as lucky as she'd thought.

Carrie chewed her lip, studied the computer screen and clicked on a folder. Around one hundred files popped up. She scanned the file names, but few seemed to make any sense.

An awful feeling of familiarity swept over her. She recalled the first day she'd worked at the company, when it had operated under a different name. She'd been hired as supervisor of the call centre in spite of the fact that she had no relevant qualifications. She'd soon found herself entirely out of her depth.

Most puzzling and frustrating of all had been the call centre's manual for dealing with complaints. The steps had seemed to lead customers around in a circle rather than dealing with the complaint.

The files on the computer screen might have made more sense than the complaints manual if Carrie had the slightest understanding of businesses or accounting or sales figures or staffing protocols or manufacturing agreements. The truth was, she probably had a better comprehension of the pheromone language of her alien managers in her other job as a Transgalactic Intercultural Community Crisis Liaison Officer. In other words, a smidgen more than nothing.

Carrie sighed again and closed the screen. Should she give up the idea of managing the company and leave? If she slipped out the back door maybe no one would notice. She loved her new expensive house and car, but were they really worth the trouble and responsibility of running a company? She fondly recalled her little flat where she'd previously been perfectly content living with her dog, Rogue, and her cat, Toodles. If she found a simple job, like dog walker or ice-cream seller, she might be happier, if poorer.

She gave a sudden sneeze and noticed that her throat was sore. Great. To add to her problems, she had a cold.

As had become her habit when she didn't know what to do, she decided to ask her best friend for advice. Carrie went out, nearly bumping into her personal assistant, Alice, who was holding a full mug.

"Oh, sorry," said Alice. "I was just bringing your tea."

"Great. Thanks. Just put it on my desk."

Carrie went through the outer office where Alice sat and then down the stairs.

Alice hadn't asked her if she wanted any tea. Carrie wondered if she had one every morning. As far as Alice was concerned, Carrie had been the company owner for years. But Carrie herself was living a new time line that had been created by something that happened during her previous assignment with the Transgalactic Council. She hadn't lived those years that Alice had known her and she had no memory of them. Technically, she was the same person, so Alice probably wouldn't notice anything too different, but Carrie worried about slipping up in some other way that might make Alice think she was losing it. Just thinking about it all made her head spin.

Rob from Accounts passed her in the corridor. All the people working at Carrie Hatchett Enterprises seemed to be the same ones she remembered.

"Hi Rob," she said cheerfully.

"Morning, Ms. Hatchett."

Ms. Hatchett? Hadn't her previous self told the staff

to call her Carrie? That would be one thing she would change.

The call centre department was on the other side of the building. It was reassuring to see as she made her way over, that everyone seemed to be working happily. No disasters yet.

As she stepped into the call centre, Carrie's first impulse was to check who was sitting at the supervisor's desk—her previous spot. A woman around her own age was there, speaking into a head mic and looking very harassed. *Not surprising.*

Her friend Dave was sitting with his back to her. No lights were flashing on his console, which meant he had no calls waiting. He was playing a game on his phone to pass the time. When Carrie touched him on his shoulder, he jumped and quickly shoved the mobile into his pocket.

"Oh, it's you," he said, relieved, when he saw who had disturbed him. He spoke quietly. "What are you doing here?"

"I wanted to talk to you about something."

"Huh? Why didn't you call me? Don't you know my extension number? Reception would have put you through."

Carrie flushed a little. "I didn't think of that."

"Maybe we should go outside to talk," said Dave.

"Good idea. Bring your umbrella though. It looks like rain."

***

Smokers were hanging around the back door of Carrie

Hatchett Enterprises. They melted away when Carrie appeared with Dave. If she did want to secretly walk out, she would need a different escape route. Dave opened his large black umbrella as thick drops of rain began to fall.

"You know," he said, "it might be better if you didn't approach me like that when we're at work. You're the boss now and I'm just one of your call centre workers. People will think it's weird."

"Yeah, maybe you're right. Yet another downside to my surprise ownership of this company. Dave, you've got to help me. I don't know if I can do this. I don't know the first thing about running a business."

"I'm sure you can learn, if you put your mind to it. You can be really smart sometimes."

Carrie put her hands on her hips. "What do you mean, *sometimes*?"

The rain began to pour down.

"I just mean..." Dave coughed. "I mean, that, sometimes, you..."

Carrie looked up at him from under frowning eyebrows.

"Oh stop it," he said. He gave her a shove, pushing her out into the rain.

"Hey," Carrie exclaimed as her untameable hair became instantly wet. Chuckling, she stepped under the umbrella again. "Seriously, I could do with some of that smartness right now. I don't even feel like going back to my office. I mean, what am I supposed to do there? What *do* company owners do all day? I've never even

7

thought about it. Never thought I'd have to."

"Actually...I don't know either."

They both paused as they tried to figure out the answer to the problem.

"Maybe they have meetings?" Dave offered.

"Maybe. But if I call a meeting, I'll have to speak to everyone as if I know what I'm doing. It won't be long before they all figure out that isn't true." Carrie shivered. The rain was cold and she'd come out without her coat. "I'm worried that if I try to do anything, I'm going to mess up. Everyone's relying on me for their livelihoods. I can't take the risk. I might make a disaster of everything. I'm just going to have to sell the company."

"Don't do that," Dave exclaimed. "That's the worst thing you could do."

"Why?"

"Carrie, every boss I've ever worked for has been bad. Just nasty and egotistical people who behaved terribly towards their staff. Now that *you* own the company, we have someone nice to work for. Someone who actually cares about us as people. Remember what it was like working here before we changed the time line?"

Carrie did remember, and her mind returned to the young woman now sitting where she used to sit. She would be fielding complaints and sending customers down a rabbit hole of never-ending frustration until they finally gave up. Maybe she could do something to make her job easier. Before going on her last

Transgalactic Council assignment, she'd put together a list of suggestions to her former boss intended to increase customer satisfaction. She could recall most of them.

"Thanks, Dave. That's really kind of you to say that. And it's true. I do care about the people who work here. In my previous life, they were my friends, and as far as I'm concerned, they still are. Maybe there are some things I can do to make Carrie Hatchett Enterprises a great place to work." Carrie sneezed.

"Bless you," said Dave. "Maybe we should go inside? It sounds like you've got a cold, and my boots are getting ruined."

"You and your boots. All right. Come on then."

At the door, Dave shook out his umbrella and placed it in the corner to dry. They went in different directions down the corridor, Dave returning to the call centre and Carrie returning to her office. She felt calmer after her talk with her best friend. For the moment, she had something concrete to do. She would look up the complaints procedure and try to improve it. Customers were constantly complaining about the items of equipment that her company sold. It was a wonder how it survived. She had never understood exactly what they made or what the things did. Maybe finding out would be her next step.

Maybe she could learn to be the boss of a company after all. She remembered the tea Alice had made her and hoped that it wasn't cold. Then she realised that if it was, all she had to do was ask Alice to make her another cup.

When she arrived at her outer office, however, Alice didn't look as though she was in the mood for making tea. The woman looked frantic, in fact.

"Ms. Hatchett," she exclaimed. "Thank goodness you're back. Your phone's been ringing off the hook. First it was customers, then shop owners, and then it was the police. They're on their way."

"The police? What's happened?"

"All the tools and parts we sell have been going crazy and attacking people."

CHAPTER TWO

By the time the police left, Carrie wasn't sure how she'd managed to escape arrest. She'd never had to deal with them before, even in her younger, wilder years. Their endless probing questions had made her fearful, but she'd answered as honestly as she could. She really didn't have any idea how or why the products supplied by Carrie Hatchett Enterprises had suddenly become involved in numerous accidents across the nation.

What had perhaps worked in her favour was the fact that the police seemed to discredit some of the incredible stories that Alice had heard from customers. The people phoning in had said that the tools and equipment had actually come to life. What was more, they'd said that, after committing various violent acts, the appliances had actually run away.

The police hadn't asked her about anything like that. They'd said that Carrie Hatchett products were faulty

J.J. GREEN

and dangerous. They'd brought in inspectors to check her company's safety compliance in its manufacturing standards. Thankfully, the earlier Carrie had been responsible and thorough, and the preliminary inspection had found nothing wrong.

Yet she felt frazzled and stressed by the time the police and inspectors finally departed. The staff had also gone home for the day, leaving the phones continuing to ring. The voice mail would be full by morning.

Carrie said good bye to the security guard and went out to her car. It was the first moment she'd had to herself since before chatting with Dave that morning. She suddenly felt very tired and hungry. She got in her car and started it up, promising herself that she wouldn't check any messages on her land line when she arrived home. She wouldn't put it past the angry customers to find out her home phone number and call her there.

She wouldn't blame them if they did. The equipment her company made had caused terrible problems. But she needed some time alone to think and figure it all out. She had already issued an immediate recall of everything manufactured by Carrie Hatchett Enterprises. It would bankrupt the company, no doubt, but it was the least she could do.

Carrie drove around the corner into her street, and her heart sank. The press had found out where she lived. A horde of reporters, cameramen and photographers were hanging around her house. They were even in her garden, trampling her flowers.

12

For a split second, she considered doing a U-turn and driving to Dave's house. With luck, no one would spot her and follow her there. But then she remembered Toodles and Rogue. They would be waiting for her and their evening meal.

Resigned, Carrie continued driving to her house. She beeped her horn when she reached her driveway. The press were obstructing it, but a gap appeared as they caught sight of her and rushed forward. Carrie eased her car through the space, trying to avoid hurting anyone. Some of them were being foolishly unsafe in their eagerness to snap a photo of her. The reporters were shouting questions through her car's windows with their faces pressed up against the glass.

Carrie put on her handbrake and turned off her engine. She grabbed her handbag and pushed open her door against the weight of bodies.

"Let me out."

She entered the melee and began forcing a path through the men and women.

"Ms. Hatchett, are you aware how many people have been injured by your equipment?" a voice shouted. "How much compensation will you be paying the victims?" asked another. "Do you expect a custodial sentence?" asked a third.

Her handbag tight under her arm. Carrie inched through the crowd. She finally made it to her front door. Stepping inside her home, she turned to face the jostling men and women. "No comment." She shut the door and locked it.

Carrie ran to her windows, ignoring an over-excited, barking Rogue, and closed all her curtains and blinds. Meanwhile, her doorbell was ringing incessantly. After investigating the device for a minute or two, she figured out how to disconnect it. The ringing stopped.

She flopped onto her sofa and put a hand over her eyes. Just as she was about to burst into tears Rogue jumped up next to her. He licked her face.

"You aren't allowed up here," Carrie said. She cuddled him. Something soft and warm had settled on her lap. She stroked Toodles, who purred and rubbed her head against Carrie's hand. "What would I do without you two? Ah...ah...atchoo!" She groaned and found some tissues so she could blow her nose.

After feeding her pets, Carrie went upstairs to her home office and turned on her computer. She wanted to find out what might have gone wrong with her company's products. The idea that they could suddenly come alive was preposterous, yet that was what people had said.

She checked the news websites, which showed video footage from CCTV cameras and mobile phones. In one of the videos, a man was shown running down a tree-lined street pursued by a tripod of some kind. The object was running along on its three legs, slowly gaining on the terror-stricken man. In another video, a woman was engaged in a fight with a snapping metal box-like structure. She was bashing it with a metal spatula and fending it off.

Carrie clasped her hands under her chin and peered

at the screen. There was something terribly familiar about what she was seeing, but she could hardly believe her suspicion. Could it be true? Could her work with the Transgalactic Council have become dreadfully entwined with her life on her home planet?

Briefly, she wondered if she was only finding a convenient scapegoat for what was happening. The explanation that there might be another reason for what was going on, other than her company's incompetence, was tempting. But, no—the resemblance to what she'd seen so often in her role as a Liaison Officer was unmistakable.

The light on her mobile was flashing. Another call. She had turned off the sound. Carrie was about to ignore it like all the rest when she saw that the call was from Dave.

"Hi," she said as she answered. "Have you seen the videos on the news? Are you thinking what I'm thinking?"

"I absolutely am. But more importantly, are you okay? I saw you on the news too, fighting through all the reporters. Are they still there outside your house?"

"I haven't looked recently. Probably."

"You poor thing. The police should give you protection."

"I'm not contacting *them*. I thought they were going to arrest me earlier. Anyway, it doesn't matter. I can deal with the media. Back to the Carrie Hatchett products going berserk. Shall I contact our Council manager or do you want to?"

"You do it. You're the only one who can pronounce her name."

"I'm not sure about that, but I'll give it a try. I'll call you back, okay?"

Carrie went to find her Transgalactic Intercultural Community Crisis Liaison Officer toolkit and took out her translator, which also worked as a communication device. She silently wished it was her former manager, Gavin, she was about to contact. But he'd been dismissed from the Transgalactic Council for reckless and dangerous behaviour. The fact that his heroic act had saved Carrie and Dave from being trapped in the past didn't matter to the Council, who expected their managers to behave sensibly.

Carrie also wished she could speak to Gavin because his name was a hell of a lot easier to pronounce than Errruorerrrrrhch, who was her current manager and Gavin's off-again-on-again partner as well as mother of his more than one hundred children. Carrie could say most of Errruorerrrrrhch's name, but both she and Dave struggled with the final syllable.

"Errruorerrrrrh," she said into her translator. "Errruorerrrrrh." If Carrie didn't pronounce the name correctly, the communication wouldn't go through. When no reply came for the second time, she raised her voice and said, "Errruorerrrrrh*ch*." A tiny spray of spittle flew out of her mouth.

The manager replied, "Transgalactic Intercultural—"

"Errruorerrrrrh," said Carrie. "Please listen. We have a crisis here on Earth. Mechanical aliens are attacking us. I think it's something to do with the placktoids."

CHAPTER THREE

Carrie and Dave put on their fluorescent orange jumpsuits at Carrie's home. They were about to travel via transgalactic gateway to a Transgalactic Council starship where Errruorerrrrrhch would listen to their report.

Dave came into Carrie's kitchen to wait with her for the gateway to open. It would appear in its usual place beneath her kitchen sink. Not for the first time, Carrie wondered how, despite their hideous uniform, Dave always managed to look attractive and stylish. When Carrie was wearing her jumpsuit she avoided mirrors. Even though she'd finally asked for a size that fitted her, having given up on the hope that she would lose enough weight to fit into the too-small uniform she'd first selected, the clothes still emphasized her pot belly and dumpy legs.

"Is something wrong?" Dave asked. "Are you worried

about the placktoids? The Council sealed them in the past with a time shield, remember? I'm sure Errruorerrrrh will have an answer. And it doesn't look as though your products have seriously hurt anyone yet."

"Yet," Carrie repeated. "I am worried about that, but...oh, never mind. It isn't important. Don't you hate these uniforms, though? I mean, they're such an ugly colour and completely unflattering. On me, anyway. I'll never forget when I had my interview and Gavin said I could take a uniform. I was imagining something cool, like an inter-galactic traveller *should* wear. Something in black and silver." She gazed down at her stubbornly pudding-like belly ruefully. No amount of training in her favoured martial art, bagua zhang, ever seemed to have any effect on it. She had even stopped eating biscuits, though that wasn't entirely by choice—Dave could polish off a tinful in one sitting, as he did whenever he visited.

"Carrie," Dave said.

"Don't you think it would be great if we could wear capes?" Carrie asked him, still looking down at her stomach. "You know, like superheroes do?"

"Carrie," Dave said, "the gateway's opening."

The cupboard door was swinging open, revealing swirling green mist.

"Here I go," said Dave, diving at the gateway. It sucked him in.

After a few tries, Dave had learned to travel via gateway with some aplomb. Carrie still always managed to bump her head at the other end. She already had a headache from her cold, so she was determined that this time would be different. She guessed that if her feet went in first, she wouldn't hit her head.

Pleased that Dave had gone and therefore wouldn't witness what she was about to do, Carrie lay down on her back and lifted her feet in the air. She wriggled towards the spinning green space bottom first. As she inched nearer, she felt the tug of the gateway's gravity field. Her plan was working. Finally, she would land on her feet in a graceful and dignified manner.

Rogue came bounding into the kitchen and began barking at the gateway.

"Go away," Carrie exclaimed. "Rogue, bed."

Carrie's canine pet had once accidentally travelled via gateway to an alien planet. If he were to arrive on a Transgalactic Council starship, Errruorerrrrrhch would be very displeased. Though the Council manager had softened towards Carrie since the first time they'd worked together, she was a very strict, by-the-book boss. She was definitely not a fan of Carrie's often somewhat unorthodox methods.

The tug of the transportation device had lifted Carrie and she was floating around thirty centimetres above her kitchen floor. Rogue gripped her uniform shoulder with his teeth. He began pulling her away from the gateway.

"Rogue, stop it. You're a very naughty boy."

The dog was growling at the green mist, no doubt thinking it was an enemy attacking his mistress. Carrie squirmed, trying to both free herself from her dog's grasp and push him out of danger of following her. With an extra-strong twist, she managed to unlock Rogue's toothy grip on her uniform and at the same time push him away.

The dog slid backwards across the tiled floor, and Carrie turned a somersault in mid-air just before entering the green mist. The next thing she knew, she was sliding headfirst into the creamy ceramic wall of the Transgalactic Council starship.

"Ow." Carrie rubbed the top of her head as she sat up.

"What took you so long?" Dave asked. "I was wondering if you were going to make it before the gateway closed."

"Nothing," Carrie replied grumpily, still rubbing her head. She got to her feet. "Let's go find Errruorerrrrrh's office."

Carrie had improved in at least one aspect of her job in the time she'd been working as a Transgalactic Intercultural Community Crisis Liaison Officer: she could now read the weird symbols and signs that decorated the entrances to the Council's rooms. Or, rather, she'd developed an intuitive understanding of them.

If she'd been asked for a translation, she would have said the symbols signified several ideas. Some of them were obvious and rational to humans, like the ship's deck and room number and the purpose of the room. Other signs related to the emotions surrounding the things that went on inside a room. So a symbol might mean something like 'expect surprises' or 'if you're in a depressive state of mind, avoid this place if possible'. Some symbols were to do with the amount of time the room was occupied on average, and others described the style of the room. To Carrie's eyes, all the rooms seemed much the same style—quite bare and boring— but she guessed that the 'style' might have something to do with pheromone signatures.

"Here we are," she announced when they arrived at Errruorerrrrrhch's meeting room.

"Are you sure?" Dave asked, peering at the black symbols and intermittently flashing lights that surrounded the door.

"Yes." Carrie gently laid her palm on the smooth surface and it melted away. The door had either been pre-programmed with her DNA or it was general access.

They were in the right place. Errruorerrrrrhch's bulky insectoid figure loomed within.

Dave hesitated on the threshold. "She hasn't had any more kids, has she?"

Carrie looked closely. The Council manager wasn't swarming with a hundred or so mini-versions of herself.

"No," she said. "You're fine. Come on."

"Transgalactic Intercultural Community Crisis Liaison Officer Hatchett," Errruorerrrrrhch said as Carrie and Dave went in. "And Transgalactic Intercultural Community Crisis—"

"Hi," Dave said.

"Errruorerrrrrh," said Carrie. "The Council has to help Earth. Some things like the placktoids are running amok. We have to do something."

The giant insectoid alien's antennae quivered. "I have seen some news reports from Earth that give me cause for concern, but I am not convinced that what you say is accurate. We must investigate what is happening on your home planet and discover what exactly is causing the crisis if we are to respond appropriately."

"They're like placktoids," Carrie said. "What else do you need to know?"

"And what evidence have you drawn upon in order to arrive at your conclusion?" Errruorerrrrrhch asked.

"Evidence?" Carrie exclaimed. "The evidence of my own eyes. Don't you believe me? I am pretty experienced in this area, if you remember."

"I am not denying your experience," said Errruorerrrrrhch, "only—"

"Then why won't you believe me? The people of Earth need Transgalactic Council help, and they need it now. And we need the Unity. We need troops. Soldiers. Lots of them. Before something terrible happens."

"Carrie," Dave said, placing a hand on her arm.

She removed it. "Don't try to calm me down. This is important."

"Transgalactic Intercultural Community Crisis Liaison Officer Hatchett," said Errruorerrrrrhch, "I should not need to remind you that it was yourself and your partner who were instrumental in locking the placktoids into the past history of their home planet. In addition, while I am not denying that the mechanical beings on the news reports on Earth do resemble placktoids, they are not identical. Therefore, it would seem that there is more to this problem than appears on the surface. As I mentioned, we need to make a thorough assessment of the situation to determine the most appropriate course of action."

"We don't have time for assessments," squeaked Carrie. "We need to act now before something terrible happens."

"Another consideration is the fact that the majority of Earth's population is unaware of the existence of alien life. Earth has not yet invented interstellar travel and therefore it is not a full member of the Transgalactic Council. You must understand that we have strict protocols we must follow when introducing a new species to the rest of intelligent life in the galaxy. We have learned from experience that failure to follow the protocols can cause terror and panic and result in damaging economic upheavals and civil unrest. Sending Unity troops to Earth in response to these incidents is an action the Council will only take as an absolute last resort."

"That's ridiculous!" Carrie could hardly believe what Errruorerrrrrhch was saying. "We're being invaded by some kind of alien killer robots and you don't want to send in Unity troops because they might frighten people?"

Errruorerrrrrhch was silent for a moment. "I understand why you are emotionally volatile, yet that does not change the fact that your extreme reaction to my decision may cause you to be unreliable and ineffective. Your partner may not provide enough of a balancing effect on your behaviour. I think it best that I assign a third Council operative to this task. This individual is also familiar with Earth's geography and politics."

Carrie groaned.

"Please return now," Errruorerrrrrhch said. "The operative I plan to assign will be in touch shortly. We will continue to monitor the situation on Earth. I will also dispatch a small company of Unity soldiers to aid with the location and extraction of these mechanical creatures. To avoid alarming humans they may come in contact with, I will assign only humanoid troops. They will be instructed to keep their visors closed while in front of the public to avoid causing alarm."

CHAPTER FOUR

Carrie sat on her sofa at home, resting her elbow on the armrest and her chin in her hand. She was glumly flicking through the channels on her television and blowing her nose every so often. Many of the TV channels were providing regular updates on the 'rampaging robots crisis' as the media had named it. Scenes from all over Britain showed equipment manufactured by Carrie Hatchett Enterprises coming to life and attacking the nearest humans before escaping.

Where the machines were going, no one seemed able to find out, but reports from France and the Netherlands indicated that they were spreading overseas. Was their plan to invade the entire globe?

Carrie was upset, and for two reasons. Firstly, Errruorerrrrrhch had been absolutely correct that the mechanical beings that were attacking Earth's citizens were not placktoids. The creatures had undoubtedly

26

been manufactured by her company. The police had confirmed it, but it was a fact that she'd been avoiding. She felt responsible, and that had caused her to blame the placktoids.

The second thing that was bothering her was Errruorerrrrrhch's decision to assign another local operative to the problem. In spite of all her hard work and success, Errruorerrrrrhch still didn't trust her. If she were to be brutally honest with herself, the manager's decision might have had something to do with her outburst aboard the Council starship. Dave had even mumbled something alluding to that fact when they'd returned.

The only thing worse than not being trusted was suspecting that it was your own fault.

Carrie changed the television channel to the BBC. It was midday and time for a news update.

"The rampaging robots crisis continues," said the announcer. "The Metropolitan Police were alerted to a family of four who had been held hostage in their council flat by an electric bilge plunger for three days. The father, grandmother and two boys aged four and six had survived on leftover pizza, chewing gum and a packet of Garibaldi biscuits. The police managed to distract the bilge plunger long enough to allow the family to escape, but they lost sight of the electrical device in the confusion. It was last seen heading towards Piccadilly Tube Station."

Accompanying video footage showed the family running across a street, their heads down, while helicopters circled overhead. In the background, a large, upright, metallic object could be seen disappearing into a crowd of onlookers.

Carrie tutted. Couldn't someone have tried to catch it? But then again, she understood how strange and alarming it was when mechanical objects moved with a will of their own. And if any of the bystanders had tried to prevent the bilge plunger's escape, they might have been hurt.

The announcer paused. She touched her ear bud and listened intently. She looked up at the screen. "We have some breaking news. More out-of-control mechanical devices have appeared aboard an intercity train travelling between Northampton and Birmingham. Witness reports say the robots burst out of one of the train's toilets, causing fear and panic among the passengers. Someone pulled the emergency cord, and when the train stopped, the robots tore their way out of the train, ripping the doors off their hinges. The crisis is continuing, with more and more devices miraculously emerging from the toilet. Excuse me one moment." The announcer paused again and listened to a message. "I believe we have a video recorded on a mobile phone at the scene only minutes ago."

She looked off screen at a monitor.

A jerking, swaying video appeared, shot in vertical, of a train interior. It was full of people running, screaming and shouting. Between the moving, blurred shapes and motions of the holder of the mobile trying to escape the scene, it was difficult to discern anything clearly. But a grinding, squeaking noise could be heard. It was a noise that froze Carrie's heart.

The person shooting the video seemed to escape immediate danger as the movements became less jerky and the sounds of panic quietened. The view the phone was recording swung around to the train window. Trundling, hopping and skimming above the green fields outside the train moved a procession of beings Carrie had no trouble recognizing. There was no doubt in her mind. These were the real thing: plactoids.

After all her self-doubt, Carrie's suspicions had been correct. Plactoids *were* invading Earth. The devices that her company made had to be tied up with the invasion somehow.

The horrible grinding and squealing she heard earlier in the video had been the sound of the plactoids' language that they used when they weren't communicating electronically.

Carrie picked up her phone to call Dave about this latest development, but then she paused. Why were the plactoids arriving aboard a train? They had stolen gateway technology before being locked in the past and had been using it to travel the galaxy, but she hadn't heard of gateways aboard moving objects. A train toilet seemed an unnecessarily difficult portal to open.

She breathed in sharply. When she had returned from her assignment on Dandrobia, the gateway had opened aboard an intercity train. She'd guessed that the two charming dandrobians who had escaped to Earth during her mission had tampered with the toilet to make it work as a gateway opening. That had to be it. The plactoids and dandrobians had worked together to plot a galactic takeover, and the plactoids were appearing through the entrance the dandrobians had created. But how had the plactoids escaped the time shield the Council had put down?

Carrie's phone buzzed. Dave was calling. As she went to press the screen to accept the call, the terrible squealing and grinding from the television increased. She wouldn't be able to hear Dave speak, so she picked up the TV remote to lower the volume. Pressing the button had no effect. If anything, the noise seemed to increase.

It was very odd. On the TV screen, the video didn't show any plactoids nearby.

Carrie accepted Dave's call anyway. "Wait a minute," she said loudly. "I can't hear you." She turned off the television. The noise still didn't stop.

Dave was shouting something but Carrie couldn't make out what it was. He was saying something about 'out'.

"Hold on," Carrie yelled. "It's too noisy in here. I'll have to go outside."

She went to her living room door and with each step she took, the facts of what was happening hit her.

The escaped dandrobians had enabled the train toilet to open gateway portals.

Plactoids had arrived on the train.

The escaped dandrobians had lived in Carrie's old flat, which had a gateway portal beneath her kitchen sink.

The dandrobians had as good as confessed to tampering with Carrie's gateway portal.

The same portal now existed beneath her sink in her new house...

She finally understood what Dave was saying. *Get out.*

But Toodles and Rogue were somewhere in the house. She couldn't leave them behind with the placktoids.

As Carrie stepped into her hall, a large metal shape filled the kitchen doorway, blocking the light from the window. It filled the door frame. It was too big to fit through the door so it started forcing itself against the surrounding wall. In the hall the wallpaper ripped, plaster crumbled and bricks began to bulge.

"Toodles," Carrie shouted above the placktoids' dreadful sounds. "Rogue! Where are you?"

Rogue hadn't quite forgiven Carrie for pushing him away when he'd tried to save her from the scary green mist. He'd been sulking in the spare room, sleeping on the bed and looking at Carrie with reproachful eyes whenever she went in to coax him out. The last time Carrie had seen Toodles, she'd been basking in a spot of sunlight in the porch.

A patch of bricks broke free and tumbled to the floor. Red and white dust rose in a cloud.

Carrie threw open her inner front door. Toodles was curled into a corner of the porch, frightened of the loud noises. Carrie thanked her lucky stars that, her cat carrier was also there. It took only a moment to put Toodles inside. She seemed grateful for the security. Now Carrie only had to get Rogue.

She leapt up the stairs, taking them two at a time. In the spare room, Rogue barked excitedly to see her and wagged his tail furiously. He'd decided to forgive her, or he'd entirely forgotten what she'd done.

"Rogue," Carrie said, "we're in terrible danger. Come on boy."

In response, Rogue jumped up at Carrie, pushing against her chest with his paws before jumping down again and running around the room.

"Rogue, this isn't the time for playing. Come on."

On his second circuit of the room, Carrie managed to grab the dog's collar. She pulled him out of the room while he bounced beside her good-naturedly. At the top of the stairs, Carrie stopped dead. The placktoid had succeeded in breaking out of the kitchen and was in her hall. It was scraping along the walls heading for the front door. And Toodles.

"Oh no you don't," Carrie shouted. No one and nothing, not even murderous mechanical monsters, came between her and her pets.

Lifting Rogue into her arms, she raced down the stairs and jumped onto the top of the placktoid. The mechanical alien was two metres or more tall, but Carrie leapt down from it, landing heavily on her hall carpet. She was right next to her inner front door.

Putting her dog down on the floor, she said, "Car" to him before opening the door. Rogue ran through into the porch, Carrie followed and she closed the door just in time. The frame shuddered as the placktoid hit it.

She grabbed Toodles' carrier and opened the outer door. Outside, her car was in the driveway. The street looked normal, as if mechanical monsters hadn't just appeared from across the galaxy in one of the homes.

Her pets safely in her vehicle, Carrie started the engine and pulled out into the road. As she sped away, she tried to think of somewhere to go. She couldn't take them to a hotel. She didn't know any local ones that accepted pets. Her family lived far away, and she needed to remain in Northampton to help with the crisis.

There was only one place she could think of where she and her pets would be welcome. Dave wouldn't mind some company for a while.

CHAPTER FIVE

Carrie stopped her car to search for her phone. She wanted to tell Dave that she'd escaped with her pets and they were all okay. She also wanted to tell him they were coming to stay for a while. But she couldn't find her phone anywhere. She must have dropped it in her rush to grab Toodles and Rogue and escape from the placktoids.

Carrie pulled out into the traffic once more, telling Rogue to sit still. He remained over-excited, apparently having no idea what he'd just escaped. Toodles was on the back seat in her carrier, her deep orange eyes staring between the bars.

"We're going to see Uncle Dave," Carrie told her pets. "We're going to live with him until it's safe to go home, so you must both be very good. Which means, Toodles..." Carrie glanced into the back seat through her rear view mirror. "...no scratching his furniture and no hacking up hair balls on his carpets. And Rogue..." She flicked her eyes to the dog, who was trembling with excitement. "...No climbing on the sofa or the beds and no sneaking food off the table. Understand?"

Rogue snuffled and gave a sharp bark. It sounded like he was saying yes, but he was probably only happy to be travelling in the car.

Carrie gave a small shake of her head. Maybe taking her pets to Dave's flat wasn't such a good idea. But where else could she go? Dave was a good friend. She was sure he wouldn't mind.

But when they arrived at Dave's flat, he didn't answer the door. Carrie rang the doorbell several times before realising he must have gone out to find her. He'd probably gone to her house. Carrie hated to think what the placktoids had done to it since she'd left. Should she drive back and meet him there?

She would have to take Toodles and Rogue down in the lift and back to her car. Maybe she should wait for Dave there at his flat. If she went home he might have left by the time she arrived and they would miss each other. She should stay at the flat. He would have to come home eventually. On the other hand, she didn't want him to worry about her unnecessarily.

As Carrie was trying to decide what to do, the neighbour's door opened and an old woman looked out. "Are you looking for Dave? He isn't home. He went out a while ago. He might not be back for ages."

"Oh, thanks."

"Would you like to come in and have a cup of tea

while you wait?"

"Thanks, but I'm not sure what to do," said Carrie. "I think he's gone out to look for me, but I don't have a way to contact him to tell him I'm here.."

"You don't have his phone number? I think I've got it here somewhere. Come in and I'll see if I can find it."

"I don't have a phone either."

"Oh, well, I definitely have one of those. Come in, dear, come in. What a lovely dog you have. What's his name? And is that a cat? Maybe you'd like some Lemsip? You don't look very well."

Carrie went inside Dave's neighbour's home with her pets and sat in a straight-backed armchair while the woman made some tea. After bringing Carrie a cup, she disappeared to search for Dave's phone number. Carrie occupied herself by keeping Rogue relatively still and trying to calm Toodles by stroking her through the bars of her carrier. The cat had started to miaow and the sound was becoming more and more plaintive.

"Here it is," said the woman, returning to the room. She handed Carrie a white contact card with Dave's details. Carrie hadn't known Dave had contact cards. The man was unbelievably organised.

"The phone's over here," the woman said. "I only have the old-fashioned type I'm afraid."

She wasn't joking. Her phone was the first home telephone with a dial that Carrie had seen for a long while. She dialled Dave's number. When he answered, Carrie's heart was warmed by the relief in his voice when he heard she was safe.

"I was already on my way back," he said. "I'll see you in a minute."

Carrie said goodbye and replaced the receiver in its cradle.

"Is he coming home?" the old woman asked. "That's good. He's such a lovely young man. He always helps me with my shopping and checks on me every day, just to make sure I'm all right."

"That's nice," said Carrie. "Dave's great. I really like him."

"Yes, such a shame he's single." The old woman sighed. "He'd make someone a lovely husband. He deserves to find a nice girl and settle down."

"Oh," Carrie said, surprised. "Oh, I, er...I don't think he's going to do that." Didn't the woman know Dave was gay? It wasn't like he made a secret of it. Maybe his neighbour knew but she didn't approve. Carrie hoped she hadn't got the idea that she was a potential girlfriend.

"Well why not?" the woman asked. "We only get one life. What's the point in spending it alone? You seem like a nice girl. And he's a very handsome young man. Haven't you considered making a play for him? He might be interested, you know. Men are shy about these things."

"I...er...no. I really don't think..." Carrie didn't know what to say. It wasn't up to her to put Dave's neighbour straight about his orientation.

But then she noticed that the old woman's eyes were dancing. She burst into loud guffaws. Dave's neighbour had been teasing Carrie. She knew all about him and she'd been deliberately putting her on the spot. Carrie began to laugh too. She'd fallen for it, hook, line and sinker.

They were both laughing so loudly they missed Dave's knock. They were still laughing when he came into the living room.

"Carrie, I'm so glad you're okay," he said. "What are you two laughing about?"

Carrie tried to catch her breath and answer him but she couldn't.

"Oh I get it," said Dave. "You've been up to your old tricks again, haven't you, Mrs. Bassett?" He shook his head. "She plays the same joke on every female friend who visits."

"She had me going for a while there," said Carrie.

"Carrie, we should talk."

They both thanked Mrs. Bassett for her hospitality and went into the hallway between the flats.

"How long have you been here?" Dave asked. "Have you seen your house? There isn't much left of it."

"It's okay," Carrie replied. "It doesn't matter. I got Rogue and Toodles out. We're all safe, and that's the important thing."

"Yes, you're right. It's only a house."

"What was happening with the placktoids? Did you see?"

"They were still arriving through the gateway when I got there," said Dave. "Crawling out of the rubble they'd created from your house. But the police and army appeared not long after, and then they stopped. They seem to understand about our defence forces and they know to stay away from them. I heard that the same thing happened at that intercity train.

"This is big," he said. "Maybe bigger than anything we've ever faced before. Or it could be just that it seems that way because now it's our home planet that's in danger."

"Yeah. We can't let Earth fall to the placktoids. We just can't. We have to figure this thing out."

"Maybe the Council operative who Errruorerrrrrh mentioned can help us."

Carrie scowled.

"Meanwhile," Dave continued. "What are you going to do? Where are you going to live with Rogue and Toodles while we fight the placktoids?"

Carrie was a little taken aback. Maybe her choice of place to stay wasn't so clear-cut after all. "Well," she began, "I can't take them to a hotel. Hotels generally don't take pets."

"What a pity," said Dave.

"Yeah. And none of my family live close by."

"Bummer."

"Yeah."

There was an awkward silence. As Dave waited for Carrie to speak, the light of understanding began to dawn on his face, quickly followed by an expression of alarm. He looked uncomfortable.

Carrie gave him a hopeful smile.

Dave's shoulders slumped. "I suppose..." He sighed.

"I suppose you could stay with me. For a while." Carrie grabbed him and hugged him. "Until you find another place," he choked.

CHAPTER SIX

"You know," Carrie said to Dave as she put the cat blanket she'd taken from Toodles' carrier on the top of his music centre, "I just realised that this is the first time I've been here. I've given you a lift home plenty of times, but I've never been inside your flat. Isn't that weird?"

Dave was sitting on his sofa, his hands on his knees. He'd been quiet while Carrie had been making her pets comfortable. A muscle in his jaw twitched. "Yeah. It's weird. Is there a reason you're putting that there?"

"Yes. Toodles likes to sleep in high places."

"Right."

"And this is such a great place," Carrie went on. "I'm surprised you don't want to show it off more. It's so stylish and neat and tidy. I mean, look at this cream carpet you've got, it's immaculate. And the walls, there isn't a mark on them." She surveyed the room. "You've got a place for everything. Do you spend forever tidying up? Is that how you get it looking like this?"

"No. It's quite simple really. I just put things away as soon as I've finished with them."

Carrie nodded. "That's a great idea. It must be hard to keep it up though, day after day, week after week, when you have more interesting or important things to do."

"It's not hard at all." Dave was still eyeing Toodles' blanket. "Are you sure that's a safe place for Toodles to sleep? What if she falls down?"

"Oh, she'll be fine. Don't worry about her." Carrie loved how Dave was concerned about her pets.

"But how will she get up there?"

"She'll find a way. She's a cat." Carrie pointed at Dave's bookcase. "She'll probably jump onto that, then the back of the armchair, then the TV. Or another route. Cats are clever like that." She looked around for somewhere for her dog to sleep. "Can I borrow some old towels for a bed for Rogue? I left his at the house."

"I don't have any old towels," said Dave.

"Blankets?"

"Nope."

"An old duvet?"

"I don't have an old anything," said Dave. "I throw old things away or take them for recycling."

"Hmmm. That's a problem. Where's Rogue going to sleep?"

"There's a bigger problem. Where are you going to sleep? This is a one-bedroom flat."

"Oh, don't worry about me. I can sleep anywhere."

Dave had been strangely stiff and reserved, but he softened a little then. "Carrie, what did you bring with you from your house? What have you got in your car?"

"Nothing, unless you count some empty juice cartons, crisp packets and chocolate wrappers. I think I might have a first aid kit in the boot. Why?"

"Did you even manage to grab your handbag? Have you got your purse? Driving licence? Bank cards? Council toolkit?"

Carrie was slowly shaking her head as he listed the items. "Nope. Nothing like that. I didn't have time to get them. There was a plactoid after me and more were arriving from the gateway in my kitchen. I grabbed Toodles and Rogue and bolted. You know what it's like."

"Aren't you upset that you've lost all your stuff? Nearly everything you have is gone."

"Pfff." Carrie waved a dismissive hand. "I've got everything I need right here in this room." Rogue had been nuzzling her knee, begging for cuddles. She squatted down and ruffled his neck, screwing up her eyes as he reciprocated her love by licking her face. "I'll have to pop down the shops and buy some pet food. And maybe a bed for Rogue." She made a mental note to buy some headache tablets too. Her head was pounding.

The doorbell rang. Dave got up to answer it. He returned with a visitor, who was someone depressingly familiar. When Errruorerrrrrhch had mentioned another Council operative on Earth, Carrie should have guessed right away who she meant. Following Dave into his living room was half-human, half-dandrobian Belinda.

Carrie smiled stiffly. After a falling out, she and Belinda had arrived at a truce at their last encounter, yet Carrie had never quite forgiven the woman for nearly hurting the Oootoon through her arrogance and neglect.

"Hi, Carrie. I'm glad you're both here. I've got some news. Errruorerrrrrhch told me the Council has responded to the arrival of the placktoids by dispatching several Unity starships. They'll be here in a few days to deal with the invaders if we can't manage to repel them ourselves. Meanwhile, the Unity company she promised will arrive by gateway tomorrow."

"I hope this won't turn into an all-out war," Dave said.

"I hope not too," Belinda replied, "but it's good to know we'll have the Unity's help if we need it."

"Let's see what we can do ourselves," said Dave. "Would you like some tea?"

"I'd love some," Belinda replied.

"Carrie?"

"No thanks. I had some at your neighbour's."

Dave went into his kitchen.

"Sorry about what happened to your house," Belinda said. "I saw the remains on the news."

"Thanks, but it's okay. It's just a house. I got my pets out safely and we'll all be fine staying with Dave for a while."

"Did you have insurance?"

"For the house? No. I never got around to buying it."

"Really? That wasn't very wise, if you don't mind me saying so."

Carrie recalled that Belinda worked as a banker as well as for the Transgalactic Council. "I'm pretty sure there aren't any house insurance policies that cover alien invasions."

"You'd be surprised what they cover and how they can be interpreted. But even if the placktoids hadn't destroyed your home, you could have had a fire or a flood or a burglary. Insurance covers all kinds of things. It's sensible to have it."

"I had placktoids bursting out of my kitchen. Not a burglary or a fire or an unfortunate meteorological event. And I don't think an invasion of mechanical aliens counts as an act of God, so—"

"Here we are," said Dave as he returned with a tray holding two mugs of tea and a bowl of sugar.

Belinda and Carrie were glaring at each other. Dave looked from one to the other before setting down the tray on the coffee table. He mumbled something that Carrie heard faintly as *Didn't take you two long*.

He sat in the middle of the sofa. Carrie sat on one side of him and Belinda sat on the other. Belinda took a mug of tea from the tray.

"No biscuits?" Carrie asked.

"Oh no," Dave replied. "I don't keep them in the house. Too unhealthy."

Belinda said, "Can you fill me in on what you've done so far about the placktoids? Have you figured out how

Carrie's products are related? I assume they are."

Carrie bristled. "It's complicated. The placktoids have somehow circumvented the time shield the Council put in place. We don't know yet what the link is with the machines my company made, but it seems likely there is one." She gasped.

"What?" Dave asked.

"That's why nothing ever worked properly," she exclaimed. "That's why we had that stupid complaints policy that led the customers in circles. We've been manufacturing obscure tools and equipment that were never intended to actually work properly. All the products were the seeds of an alien invasion."

Dave nodded. "Makes sense."

Toodles appeared at the door, rubbing her cheek against the edge as she walked in. The cat had obviously completed her assessment of the premises and found them satisfactory. Then Toodles halted and sniffed the air. Her eyes turned in the direction of the scent she'd detected. She stared at Belinda.

Her tail bushed out and all along her spine her fur stood up. A low grumble emanated from her throat, turning into a hiss. Toodles flew across the room and leapt onto Dave's bookcase. From there she vaulted onto the top of his flat screen television, which began to topple forward. Dave jumped up just in time to catch it before it fell. From the television Toodles sprang onto the music centre and landed on her blanket.

The material slid along the smooth, polished surface, carrying the cat with it. Toodles hit the wall, then tried to scramble down the gap at the back of the music centre which pushed it backward. Carrie ran to grab the centre. Toodles plummeted sideways, twisting in mid-air to land on all four paws before bolting out of the room.

Dave was holding his television. Carrie was holding his music centre. Belinda was holding her mug of tea, looking very confused.

CHAPTER SEVEN

The Unity troops were arriving through a gateway that the Transgalactic Council opened at Scotland Yard in London. Dave, Carrie and Belinda had travelled into London to be present to receive them. The Commissioner of the Metropolitan Police was aware of the existence of the Transgalactic Council and had been briefed on everything that was happening. He'd provided the alien soldiers with police riot uniforms. The helmets had darkened visors that would hide the soldiers' faces from the general public and the police officers or military personnel who might work with them.

"I'm not sure this is such a good idea," Dave said as he and Carrie watched the new arrivals exiting the gateway. The humanoid aliens were a range of colours and some of their faces were far from human. "We're used to seeing extraterrestrials, but any of these would terrify a member of the public. Besides, I'm sure our police could handle the placktoids if they were given the right weapons."

"The placktoids are a Transgalactic Council problem," Carrie countered, "and it's the Unity's job to protect Earth. I'm glad they're here and military starships are on their way. We need all the help we can get. Anyway, it's only one company. The starships carrying the full contingent won't be here for days. Maybe we can find the placktoids and make them surrender before the rest of the Unity troops arrive, and everyone can go back to their normal lives. At least these soldiers can pass as human and the public won't be alarmed by the sight of them."

"The public's already alarmed." Dave stared at Carrie. "What are you doing?"

She'd been rubbing pressure points on her nose and ears, trying to clear her stuffed-up passages. She folded her arms. "Nothing."

Despite the best efforts of the police and the army, who had also been drafted in, no one managed to find a single placktoid. They and the machines manufactured by Carrie Hatchett Enterprises seemed to have disappeared. Carrie wondered if they were all ensconced in one spot or hidden in many places, or if they were continually on the run, moving from place to place under the cover of darkness.

The problem was that the placktoids and other machines had great camouflage. All they had to do was to remain still, and any passing human would assume they were only an odd piece of abandoned equipment. Perhaps whoever noticed them wouldn't be able to tell exactly what they did, but that wouldn't matter. People were used to not understanding the purpose of unfamiliar machines. Even if the setting wasn't industrial or urban, the aliens only had to dot themselves tastefully across a green field and everyone would think they were a modern art display.

What bothered Carrie most was that she knew exactly why the placktoids were there. They clearly had a plan they had been hatching for a long time. They were in league with the dandrobians, who had set up the gateways that had allowed them in. Carrie also hadn't forgotten the map of the galaxy on the walls of the empty library on Dandrobia. It had shown a planned route with Earth at its centre. An invasion route.

Earth was only the beginning. Carrie feared for her fellow humans, who were about to become caught in a terrible galactic crisis. Most of them didn't even know aliens existed. If something didn't happen soon, they were about to have a rude and painful awakening.

Carrie had to find the placktoids, or at least figure out how they intended to carry out their plan.

Belinda came into the room.

"Hi," she said, "I'm here to oversee the Unity troops' deployment."

"I thought that was our joint role," said Carrie.

"No," replied Belinda. "Errruorerrrrrhch specifically asked me to do it. She felt I was best suited to the task due to my experience in working for the Unity."

"Hmpf," said Carrie. She had a feeling that Belinda's story wasn't quite correct. It was more likely that she'd suggested to Errruorerrrrrhch that she take the lead role. It would be just like her.

"Carrie," said Dave.

She realised she was silently staring at Belinda. "What?"

"If we aren't needed here, let's go see what else we can do."

"I suppose we should but..." Carrie's gaze returned to Belinda.

"Carrie," Dave repeated, "come on."

"Wait a minute. I was just thinking about something. Belinda, you're half dandrobian, aren't you?"

"Yes. And?" said Belinda.

"What does that mean exactly? Have you ever been there?"

"Yes, I have. My father is dandrobian. My mother and I went to visit him fairly often as I was growing up and I've been a few times as an adult. Why?"

Carrie had been about to ask Belinda if she knew about the dandrobian involvement with the placktoids, but she changed her mind. She thought only she and Dave had seen the dandrobians' silvery star map or knew that their former Council manager, Gavin, had made a recording of it. As far as anyone knew, the dandrobians weren't aware their secret had been discovered. Until they were absolutely certain of Belinda's true affiliations, it would be wiser to tell her nothing.

"Oh," said Dave. Carrie's train of thought seemed to have occurred to him too.

Carrie nudged his ankle with the toe of her shoe. His mouth closed like a trap.

Belinda's eyes narrowed. "What's going on with you two? Why are you asking about my dandrobian background?"

Belinda didn't seem to know about the connection, Carrie concluded. She'd been correct to not say anything. But what other excuse could she give for her questions? "Oh, it's, er...nothing. I was just wondering."

There was a loud knock at the door. Carrie, Dave and Belinda went out to speak to the young police sergeant waiting there. "Please come with me," the sergeant said. "There's been a development."

The three Council Liaison Officers followed the sergeant.

"Wait," Carrie said to Belinda. "Aren't you supposed to be overseeing the troops?"

Belinda scowled and flicked her auburn locks over her shoulder. Carrie gave her a wave as they left.

Upstairs in the Commissioner's office, a horrible squeaking, grinding voice was ringing out. A metal grille filled the screen of the Commissioner's computer. It was the closest thing to a face the placktoids had. At first, Carrie couldn't make any sense of the creature's noise, but then she realised she was hearing English. The placktoid was speaking her language, though listening to the sound was painful.

Carrie wished she had her Council translator, which

converted the plactoids' speech into a BBC accent. But her Council toolkit was buried under the remains of her house.

The Commissioner was pale and his expression was grave. "The announcement began a couple of minutes ago. They've hacked every broadcasting station. We're recording it."

> *And we will enslave the people of Earth as you have enslaved our kind for generations. You will suffer as our kind have suffered. You will become our tools to use as we see fit, helping us to gain control of the galaxy and bend all inferior organic life forms to our will. You will obey our every command until you are broken and discarded, destroyed and disintegrated to your essential elements.*
>
> *If you refuse, you will suffer until you obey. When the first victims die, we will take and torture more and more of you until you accept our sovereignty. Do not doubt our determination. We have generations of revenge to exact upon the people of Earth. It will be our joy and pleasure to carry out our threat.*

The screen went black. The Commissioner ran his hand through his thin, grey hair. "Never in all my years did I expect..." His words dried up. He looked searchingly at Carrie and Dave. "Do you have any idea what that creature was talking about? What on Earth does it mean, 'enslaved our kind'?"

"I'm not sure, but..." Carrie remembered her first encounter with the placktoids. The first placktoid she'd ever seen had resembled a giant paperclip. She also recalled her time aboard their starship in orbit around the planet, Oootoon. The placktoid commander, which had looked like a gigantic office shredder, had said something along the lines of the threat they had just witnessed.

Gavin had told her that the placktoids had seen videos from Earth which had shown humans using paperclips, shredders, staplers, pens and other office equipment that just so happened to appear similar to the placktoids' many forms. The aliens hadn't understood that human stationery wasn't sentient like them.

"But what?" urged the Commissioner. "Any light you can shed on this could be very helpful."

"Our television broadcasts are very popular throughout the galaxy," Carrie explained. "Aliens think we're hilarious. The placktoids saw us using stationery, which, due to some weird unfortunate random chance, looks like smaller versions of themselves. Because stationery looks like them, they think we're enslaving mini-placktoids. The announcement was telling us they plan to enslave us in the same way."

"And use us to help them take control of the galaxy," Dave added.

The Commissioner said, "I'm not sure I fully comprehend what you mean, but there's one thing I do know—this is far more serious than a civil disturbance. The Deputy Prime Minister is bringing in all the military services."

"The Deputy Prime Minister?" Carrie asked. "Don't you mean the Prime Minister?"

"The Prime Minister? You missed the first part of the message. The plactoids have kidnapped her."

CHAPTER EIGHT

Carrie and Dave remained in the Commissioner's office where they could receive reports from the army and the police as they explored all the leads they had. Carrie's cold was growing worse. She felt terrible but she didn't want to leave in the middle of a crisis.

When Belinda joined them they told her the news.

"The Prime Minister? How did the placktoids manage to snatch her right from under the noses of her security personnel?" Belinda asked. "She must be one of the most heavily guarded individuals in Britain."

The Commissioner looked rueful. "It was unfortunately very easy. We still aren't on top of the fact that this threat is like nothing we've ever dealt with before." In response to Belinda's questioning look, he added, "I have the body cam recording of a security officer who was present, if you'd like to see it."

"Yes, I would," Belinda replied.

The Commissioner typed something on his keyboard and turned the computer screen to face them.

Carrie had seen the footage already but she watched it again. It had been immediately obvious to her when she saw the video that the object next to the Prime Minister was a placktoid, but she could also see that to the untrained eye it could be mistaken for a recycling bin. Mechanical arms had appeared and lifted the Prime Minister inside almost before she or anyone else had noticed. When the machine rolled away at high speed, the officers gave chase. They didn't fire, probably because they didn't want to accidentally hit the Prime Minister. Carrie doubted that ordinary bullets would have had any effect on the placktoid. The Transgalactic Council had developed special weapons to pierce the placktoids' reinforced armour, but the British security officers couldn't be expected to know that.

The video made it clear that the officer wearing the body cam had also run after the speeding placktoid, which disappeared around a corner. When the officer rounded the same corner, the placktoid had disappeared.

"There's one thing we can look forward to," said Dave when the video came to the end and froze, "eventually, the placktoids are going to discover that our stationery isn't alive. They're going to understand that we haven't been enslaving their long-lost cousins, and hopefully they won't hate us so much."

"Maybe," said Carrie, "but I wouldn't bet on it. Those creatures are set on taking control of the galaxy. We know it because of the dandr—" She clamped her mouth shut. She'd forgotten Belinda was now with them.

"The dandrobian what?" asked Belinda.

"Nothing," said Carrie.

"I knew you two were hiding something from me. What have the dandrobians got to do with this? And why hasn't anyone told me about it?"

"It's not important," said Carrie. "It's just a guess, and anyway, you're busy organising the Unity troops. You have enough on your plate. Don't worry about it."

"If this has something to do with my father's people, I have a right to know."

"She's right," said Dave. "She does."

"Dave," Carrie exclaimed. "What if she's..." She was about to say 'spy' when she realised how ridiculous she sounded. Belinda had fought as hard against the placktoids as anyone when she'd been working with the Unity. If she was in league with her father's people, she'd had plenty of opportunities to sabotage the efforts to fight them, but she'd done nothing.

"Look," Dave said, "this stupid rivalry between you two has to stop. We have more important things to deal with at the moment."

Carrie hated it when Dave was correct. "Oh, all right." She told Belinda about her assignment on Dandrobia and the map she and Dave had discovered. She even told her about how Apate and Notos had escaped to Earth and tampered with her gateway and created another aboard a train, somehow allowing placktoids to arrive on the planet.

From Belinda's widening eyes it was obvious this was the first she had heard of any of it. She sat down. "Why didn't Errruorerrrrrhch tell me any of this?"

"I don't know," said Dave. "It does seem strange. Come to think of it, she didn't mention anything about dandrobian involvement to me or Carrie either."

"That's true," said Carrie. "Do you think she even knows?"

"Gavin recorded the map. He must have passed it on to the Council."

"But we didn't hear anything more about it after that," Carrie said.

"I have no idea what you're all talking about," interjected the Commissioner, "but if anything you know can help us retrieve the Prime Minister and make these dreadful creatures go away, I suggest that you act upon the information immediately."

Belinda stood up. "I'm going to Dandrobia to see what I can find out."

"Is that a good idea?" Dave asked. "Won't they suspect something if you arrive there right at the moment their plans are playing out? They must know you work for the Council."

"They might suspect," Belinda replied, "but they would never say anything. I'm sure you know what they're like."

Carrie did know. Only too well. She sneezed.

"If my father's people are involved, I have a duty to find out about it. Anyway, I have the perfect excuse. I haven't been to see Dad for a couple of years. He'll welcome me with open arms."

"Right. If Belinda's going to Dandrobia," said Carrie, "I'm going to my company offices."

"Why?" Dave asked. "I don't think that's very safe."

"It should be fine," said Carrie. "It isn't like the products were made there. I want to look in the company archives and I can't access them from outside. I want to see if I can find out how Carrie Hatchett Enterprises is tied up with all this. It's like Belinda said, if I'm involved with this somehow, it's my responsibility to find out about it. Maybe there's something in those archives that will give us the key to end all this."

The door burst open and the young police sergeant ran in. "Sir," she exclaimed to the Commissioner. "Another announcement from the Prime Minister's kidnappers is coming through."

The Commissioner went to his computer and activated it. The placktoid speaker's awful screeching immediately filled the room. The creature's tone was angry and it spoke so quickly Carrie could hardly make out the words. Then its voice turned slow and deadly.

"Murderers," the alien intoned. "You are all complicit in this act of aggression and violence. Humankind will pay for this atrocity it has committed against our dear lost cousins. Not one of them... Not one single individual have we found alive. You will pay for this. We will have our revenge against all of you. And first to die will be your Prime Minister. But her death will not be quick. No. That would be too merciful. We will send her to our home planet, where she will die a slow, excruciating death."

The screen went black.

"What does it mean?" asked the Commissioner. "We haven't killed any of them. We haven't even managed to find them. And what was that about their home planet? How will the Prime Minister die there?"

"I'm guessing they've discovered that stationery isn't sentient," said Carrie. "That's what it meant by their 'dear lost cousins'. They think we've killed all our stationery in retaliation for their attack."

"How long would you say the Prime Minister could survive on the placktoid planet?" Dave asked Carrie.

She remembered that hot, dry barren place only too well. When she and Dave had been sent there by the Transgalactic Council, they had water generators with them. The poor Prime Minister had nothing. "If she manages to get out of the glare of those two suns, maybe three days. That's as long as a healthy human can survive without water."

"Three days?" said Belinda. She pulled her translation/communication device from her Liaison Officer toolkit. "Errruorerrrrrhch. I need to talk to you about the dandrobian involvement in this, and I need to go to Dandrobia. Now."

"And I need to go to Carrie Hatchett Enterprises," said Carrie.

"I'll come with you," said Dave.

"No. It's better if you stay here in case there are any more developments. We can keep in touch by phone."

61

"At least the aliens aren't killing the Prime Minister immediately," said the young police sergeant. "It's lucky how the baddies never do that, isn't it?"

They all stared at her.

CHAPTER NINE

All was quiet at Carrie Hatchett Enterprises when Carrie finally arrived after driving up from London. After the firm's products had gone haywire and started attacking people, Carrie had suspended operations indefinitely and sent everyone home. She knew that eventually she would have to close the company down. It would put a lot of people out of work, which would break her heart, but she hadn't figured out an alternative.

Carrie met the security guard at the back door to the building and went inside. The corridor she walked down was dark, empty and silent. The place was strangely eerie now that no one was around. As she made her way to her office, Carrie half-expected Bob from Accounts to appear around a corner or to hear the hum of conversation from an office.

She passed Alice's vacant desk and went into her office. Rogue and Toodles looked out happily at her from photographs on her desk as she sat down. Carrie silently thanked her lucky stars for the nth time that she had been able to get them out of her house before the placktoids destroyed it.

She turned on her computer. She hadn't had much time to become familiar with all the files before the crisis had occurred. Faced with a bewildering amount of information, Carrie paused for a moment and looked out the window to the car park. She was startled. Had something stopped moving just as she'd looked out?

She stood up and went closer to the window. Hers was the only car in the car park. The security man cycled to work. Was there anything out there that might be a placktoid? Had that litter bin always been in that spot? Was the lamppost all that it seemed to be? Though the placktoids Carrie was most familiar with resembled office stationery, she'd noticed new forms in the videos she'd studied of the recent incursions.

She watched the scene for a while, but she only saw a few cars pass along the road. It was early evening. The sky was grey and sleet was beginning to fall. It was a depressing scene, placktoids or no. Carrie shivered and rubbed her arms. She gave a cough that turned into a series of them before she returned to her computer. The sooner she could get out of the place the better.

Scanning down the list of file names, she saw many terms that were obscure and mystifying. They related to the operation of the present-day Carrie Hatchett Enterprises. What she needed to find out was how the business had first begun. Another intriguing question occurred to her—how had she become its owner?

A title caught Carrie's attention: Registration details. Her company had to be officially registered, and she would be registered as the owner.

She clicked on the file and read the document. Her eyes opened wide. She had bought the company a few months previously for several million pounds. She thought back to what she'd been doing around that time. Her hand flew to her mouth. It was just after her assignment in Dandrobia. The dandrobians had popped up again. There had to be a connection.

But Carrie Hatchett Enterprises had been manufacturing its odd, shoddy products long before then. Carrie recalled Dave telling her that he'd seen many call centre supervisors come and go, unable to deal with the hordes of angry customers.

Maybe the answer lay in the identity of the previous owner.

Carrie looked up the name. Matthias Cowper. It didn't ring any bells. She put the name into an internet search engine. Only one result included that exact name. The man was an assistant producer at the BBC. Carrie frowned as she read the list of credits for documentaries he'd worked on. They were all about Hollywood celebrities or topics related to the film industry. Something tantalising niggled at the edge of her mind, but she couldn't quite put her finger on it.

Maybe a photograph of Matthias Cowper would help. She switched the search to Images, and several photographs of an extremely tall, breath-takingly handsome man appeared. Carrie didn't recognise him at all. She was disappointed. She'd thought she might be getting somewhere, but this man didn't seem to be significant in any way, yet. She would have to research his background.

She stared at the attractive face. He was probably upper middle-class, public-school educated and so on if he worked for the BBC. He was probably a bit of a—she breathed in sharply, which made her cough. The word 'luvvie' hung on the tip of her internal tongue.

Matthias Cowper wasn't human. She was sure of it. She reached for her handbag and her phone then remembered that both were lying under the rubble of her former home. What had she been thinking of when she'd said she would keep in contact with Dave by phone?

Of course. She could call him from her desk phone, but what was his number? She had no idea. It was recorded under 'Bestie' on her mobile. Carrie slapped herself on the forehead. She was sitting right in front of the records of every Carrie Hatchett Enterprises employee. She found Dave's contact details and called him.

"Hello?" he answered, sounding slightly suspicious.

"Hi," said Carrie, "it's me."

"Carrie! How are you doing? Did you find anything?"

"I did. It's not much, but it might be something. Dave, I think my company was set up by a dandrobian."

"What?" Dave's tone was incredulous. "What makes you think that?"

"I'll explain later, but can you do me a favour? Can you see what information you can find on Matthias Cowper? Anything about his past. Where he grew up, where he went to school, that kind of thing. And what he's been doing recently."

"Is this the previous owner of your company? You think he might be dandrobian?"

"That's right."

"Another escapee? In that case, information on his childhood shouldn't exist. Okay. I'll see what I can find, and I'll tell the Commissioner about him. The police will have access to records I can't search."

"Thanks, Dave. I also want to find out how on Earth I bought this place. It cost me millions. Where would I have found that kind of money? And why? But I don't know who to ask about it. Everyone but us has lived the new time line we triggered when we went into the past to defeat the placktoids. We're the only ones who remember everything as it was before."

"Maybe you could ask Errruorerrrrrh? The Council managers understand about altering time."

"Yes, maybe I'll do that. If I ever manage to say her name properly again. What's been happening there?"

"Not much. I've taken over control of the Unity troops now that Belinda's left for Dandrobia. They're working with armed police squads and army units, searching for placktoids and guarding potential targets. I won't be back at the flat until late. Aren't you going there now you've found what you were searching for?"

"No. Finding the name of the company founder was

only the first step. I want to know what went into the manufacture of the products."

"You're going to the factory?" Dave asked. "But the police said they searched the place thoroughly and didn't find anything. All the remaining stock was normal."

"How would the police know what to look for? They aren't used to dealing with homicidal sentient machines."

"Good point. But, Carrie, I have a horrible feeling about this. I don't like the idea of you going there alone. I'm sending over some Unity troops as backup."

"Okay. I'll meet them there."

Carrie hung up. She also had a bad feeling about visiting her company's factory, but she didn't want to worry Dave.

CHAPTER TEN

Carrie pulled up outside the small factory, which stood in a quiet street in Northampton. The police had tied yellow tape across the entrance. But though the place was under investigation, she still owned it. She didn't think she needed permission to go inside.

Like the offices, Carrie had closed the factory down the minute she received the news that it was her devices that were coming to life and running amok. She'd given the order to stop production, send all the workers home and lock the doors. Only the police had been into the building since.

She'd brought a spare set of keys from her office. She approached the double doors at the front, but before lifting the tape that crossed them, she hesitated. It wasn't safe for her to go in alone. A younger version of herself would have rushed ahead without thinking, but experience had finally taught her to be more cautious.

She went back to the street and scanned the front of the building. It was old. Edwardian, or Victorian even. Tall, thin, dark windows were embedded in recesses in the thick, tiled walls. Decades of city grime had turned what might once have been a cream exterior to dirty grey. Iron railings enclosed the plot, imprisoning litter that had blown in from the street.

If Carrie Hatchett Enterprises survived the placktoid invasion, Carrie would have to do something about the dirty old building.

She would look through a window while she was waiting for the Unity troops to arrive. She pushed past a scraggly scrub that was growing next to the doorstep and squeezed into the space between the railings and the building wall. A gust of wind blew, its icy fingers penetrating the seams of Carrie's jacket. The wind carried sleet with it, which wet her hair. She gave a great sneeze and scrabbled in her jacket pocket for a tissue. Carrie almost wished she was back on the placktoids' home planet. It was warm and dry there, and she had a feeling that her nasty cold would be gone within hours.

Standing on tiptoe, Carrie peered through a window pane. Metal wires were set into the glass squares, and no lights were on inside. She couldn't see a thing. Or could she? Was that a movement inside she'd seen? It was the same experience she'd had at her company offices. Or had it been a reflection in the glass from a car passing in the street?

Another gust of wind blew. Carrie coughed, a deep, hacking cough. She would have to pick up some cough syrup from a pharmacy. Or some whiskey. Or both.

She turned and scanned the street. Where were the Unity troops Dave had promised? If only she had a phone to contact him. Unless she wanted to find a payphone, she would be forced to just wait until they turned up.

Perhaps she might see inside the building better from the rear windows, where street lamps wouldn't be shining on the glass.

Carrie waded through the weeds and navigated the old, broken pavers that surrounded the factory as she went down the narrow gap between the building and its neighbour. Something shot away into the darkness as she approached. She hoped it was a cat, not a rat.

Behind the factory was an old-fashioned brick-paved yard. Cigarette butts were scattered near the back entrance, which was also sealed with police tape. In the corner of the yard stood what must have once been the workers' water closet. 'Leaned' was a better word. The little shed looked on the verge of collapse.

The windows at the back of the old factory were identical to those at the front. But Carrie had been correct—on this side, the building was in deep shadow. The little yard was also sheltered from the wind, which made it warmer and drier than the front. She would wait there for the Unity troops to help her search the place, but she would see what she could see while she waited.

Carrie went up to a high windowsill, grabbed hold of it and pulled herself up. She could view the factory interior much better from this vantage point. Tall machines loomed almost to the ceiling at the back, near where Carrie was standing. Beyond the machines, near the entrance at the front, metal shelves held stacks of boxes. Some products weren't packed. They stood on the floor, presumably abandoned by the workers who had been sent home at short notice. The cold winter light that penetrated the thick glass of the windows reflected dully on their metal surfaces.

Tired of the effort of pulling herself up, Carrie dropped to the ground.

It was odd that the products in the factory hadn't sprung to life as the others had. Carrie wondered if shipping them out or customers attempting to use them acted as some kind of trigger.

Her nose was tickling again. She gave a sneeze so forceful it threatened to expel something important from her head. Her eyes were watering. Carrie found a clean tissue to wipe them with. The packet was nearly empty. She would have to buy some more when she picked up the cough syrup. And whiskey. And peppermint schnapps. She'd heard that was good for a cold.

Where were the Unity troops?

Carrie gripped the cold tiles of the windowsill and pulled herself up again, the toes of her boots finding a little purchase against a lip of skirting that ran around the base of the wall. She gave a little gasp. The scene had changed. The devices she'd seen had moved. She was sure of it. They *were* alive after all.

She would have to watch as long as she could to see if they moved again.

A minute passed with no sign of movement from the devices. Carrie's fingers were aching and frozen. Maybe she'd been mistaken. Another minute passed with still no movement. She was almost convinced she'd been wrong.

Then they moved. Like animals coming out of hiding when they hoped a predator had gone away, the products shifted stealthily. They inched along on their metal limbs, upper parts swivelling as if looking around. They *were* sentient. They knew what they were doing. The devices must have played dead when the police were examining them.

Carrie had to tell someone. But she had no phone.

Her fingers hurt and she wanted to drop down from the window, but if she did the products might notice her and stop moving. Grimacing in pain, Carrie watched intently. What were the creatures doing? Two identical types were moving in an identical manner, mirroring each other. They moved closer then backed away. One lever rose, and the other machine raised the same lever. They pivoted on the spot, synchronised.

Carrie's fingers finally gave way and she dropped to the ground. She put her aching hands under her armpits while she processed what she'd just witnessed. She could hardly believe it. The movements weren't like the placktoids'. The devices had looked like they were performing a kind of dance.

She recalled what Gavin had told her about the plactoids. Not only were they intelligent, he'd said, they had culture. Carrie had learned through her time travel assignment that the creatures also had a long, obscure history and their own mythology. Was it possible that, when in private, they danced? For entertainment? And were the products made by Carrie Hatchett Enterprises doing the same?

Yet what Carrie had seen hadn't seemed like a fun activity. The actions had looked measured and formal, and they'd reminded her of something else. Not a dance, but a ritual. Like a…. Could it be? A connection had flashed into her mind. The devices' movements reminded Carrie of certain birds' courtship dances.

Courtship? Courtship meant… Carrie's knees went weak. It was all she could do to stop herself from sinking to the wet, icy ground. If the creatures were courting, that meant they were mating. And if they were mating, they were producing little baby devices, probably in their hundreds and thousands. Enough to take over a planet.

Was she right? Carrie recalled the vat of baby plactoids she had stumbled across aboard their starship on her first assignment. What she'd guessed about the devices' behaviour could definitely be true, but she needed to know for sure. Perhaps she was reading too much into what she'd seen.

She had to go inside the factory and investigate. It was a little risky to do it alone but the backup troops

Dave was sending had to have nearly arrived. She would only be by herself for a few minutes.

Carrie lifted the yellow tape across the back doors and tried each key in her set until she found one that fitted. Pushing open the door, she went inside.

CHAPTER ELEVEN

The factory was barely much warmer than the temperature outdoors, and though the sun had set long ago it was considerably darker. Carrie searched for the light switch. She found the panel, but no matter which switch she flicked, no lights came on. Maybe the police had cut the electricity to the place.

The devices Carrie had seen moving remained frozen in position where they had stopped mid-dance. They stood between the shelves of boxes at the front of the cavernous factory floor. They didn't look dangerous, but she recalled the video recordings she'd seen of them attacking people. Though they weren't as big as the plactoids and they didn't appear to be armed, they had plenty of hard edges and corners that could inflict painful blows.

Carrie suddenly became very aware that she had no weapons at all. Without her phone, she also had no way to call for help. She opened the back door, which had swung closed behind her, and propped it open with a metal bin. If something went wrong, she could make a hasty exit.

She went around the hulking assembly machinery and past the production lines to the front of the building. Her breath fogged in the icy air. Her nose was tickling, but she fought the urge to sneeze. The place was so still and silent, it seemed wrong or dangerous somehow to shatter the atmosphere. Not that a sneeze would give her away. The devices knew she was there. She was sure of it.

Yet as she drew closer to the boxed and loose metal products, she softened her footsteps more and more until eventually she was tiptoeing.

The devices that had been performing the courtship ritual were suspended mid-bow. Others of the same type and different products surrounded them. It was clear to Carrie now that she could see their positions close-up that, however rushed her workers had been, they wouldn't have left them scattered around as they were. The devices had moved into their current places.

But the revelation that the products could move wasn't so remarkable. What Carrie wanted to know was what they were doing there. She was sure they could have broken out of the place if they'd wanted to. Plenty others of their kind had burst out of homes and shops over the previous few days. Why had these chosen—or been commanded—to remain in the building where they were created?

Her heart racing, Carrie reached out to touch one of the devices that had danced. Would it react? Would it attack her? Her fingertips contacted the cool metal, but the thing remained still as stone.

She returned her hand to the warmth of her jacket pocket and made another visual sweep of the creatures. She felt that they were watching her. Watching and waiting. She also had a feeling they wouldn't move or give away their sentience unless she did something to provoke them. They would maintain the deception as long as they could. But why? And why here?

Perhaps she would find the answer in another part of the factory. She went across to the packing section, where the devices had been put into boxes, ready to be sent to the unfortunate customers who had ordered them.

A small sound came from behind. Carrie swung around. Nothing seemed to have moved. Perhaps it had only been the noise of traffic in the street.

Nothing seemed strange about the packing section, though Carrie considered that she had no idea how the area was supposed to look. Bins full of polystyrene packing peanuts and rolls of bubble wrap were in one corner, finished boxes were in another. Finished products in plastic bags sat around waiting to be packed.

The boxes that had been stacked, ready to be taken over to the shelves near the front entrance, had been arranged in a fort-like construction. The structure stood roughly four metres tall and wide. A whim of one of the workers, probably. Carrie smiled. It was something she might have done herself. Working in a factory had to be pretty boring. She went over to peek inside, wondering if the person or people who made it had put something in there.

The 'door' in the walls of boxes was a low hole, and light was spilling out of it. It was waist high and Carrie had to crawl on all fours to fit through it. She paused as soon as her head reached the bright interior. The floor was entirely covered in small devices, mini versions of the standard products, and portable electric lamps stood among them. It was very odd. Carrie hadn't known that her company made these toy-like items of equipment.

Except they weren't toys. They weren't miniatures. As the understanding that she'd found what she'd been looking for hit her, Carrie began to back out. Not only were her company's products mating, they were reproducing as she'd suspected. The fort wasn't the whim of an employee, it had been constructed by the devices to house their babies. It was some kind of nest. The lights were feeding the young ones, helping them to grow.

Carrie's behind hit a hard metal corner that hadn't been there when she crawled into the nursery. She gave a yelp and went forward. But the baby devices had come to life. They were coming to meet her.

She tried to twist around, but the tunnel was too narrow. There was nothing for it. She would have to use her bottom as a battering ram and force her way out against whatever it was awaiting her outside. Carrie shuffled backwards as fast as she could. Her rear cheek struck something pointed. She yelped again but kept going, pushing the thing behind her out of the way. A metallic scrape accompanied its movement as she pushed, followed by a clang as it toppled over and hit the floor.

Carrie was out of the nest. She got up and turned around. The devices that had been scattered about near the front door had made their way over. All of them, it seemed. In the distance, more were climbing out of their boxes. She was surrounded. But the ones nearest her weren't moving. Were they waiting for her to make the first move? If she left slowly and quietly, might they let her go?

Something was crawling up her trousers. Carrie kicked her leg in alarm, and a small baby device flew through the air. It hit the wall and bounced onto the floor, where it moved weakly.

That did it.

Moving in one wave, the metallic creatures surged towards her. They began hitting her with their levers and poles. The baby devices were pouring out of their nursery. Carrie spun around, swiping the little things aside with her foot while pushing away the larger devices with her hands.

"Ow. Oooh. Argh," she exclaimed as blows rained down on her legs, hips and lower back.

She was being fiercely battered. She had to get out. Yet at the same time, her nose was tickling powerfully.

She couldn't help it. She had to sneeze. *Ah...ah...ah...*A ray of moonlight shone through a high, broken window pane*...Choo!*

Her eyes and nose watering, Carrie renewed her efforts to force a path through the attacking devices. If she could make it to the back door, she might be able to escape. But it seemed very far away.

"Ouch. Ow. Stop it!"

All she seemed able to feel was sharp metal points and painful pokes. The scrabbling of a small metal creature in her hair sent her into a whirling frenzy of movement. She located the device by touch and pulled it out of her hair. Tossing it to the floor, she pushed forward, wading through the angry crowd.

She was reminded of the reporters and photographers who had harassed her when the news broke about her involvement in the emergency. She had survived that. She could survive this too.

But then a particularly heavy, hard blow hit her at the back of her knee. The blow propelled her forward and when her leg collapsed she fell down. The devices were crowded around her so closely, she fell onto them.

Hard, metal, moving objects were under her and hitting her from above. Something hit her in the face from below and she tasted blood. She tried to stand, but something else hit her forcefully on her back.

She had to get out. But whenever she tried to move upwards or forwards, the devices forced her back. Carrie grabbed the nearest one. She swung it around in a wide arc, crashing it into the others and clearing a space. It was enough room for her to stand.

Then the thing she was holding closed around her hand, pinching the skin and bone. "Owwwwwww!" She managed to pull it open. She flung it away. The placktoids surged forward once more.

Carrie was still less than halfway to the back door. She didn't think she was going to make it.

A massive bang resounded and light burst into the building. Carrie turned to see the front door had been blown off its hinges. Her ears rang. A split second after, Unity soldiers raced in. They began firing at the attacking devices, which turned towards the soldiers to attack them instead. The troops' specially designed weapons cut through their ranks.

The baby devices went scurrying back to their nursery, but the larger ones sped towards the exit at the back of the building.

Carrie fell to her knees. She was saved.

CHAPTER TWELVE

After the doctor at Northampton Hospital's Accident and Emergency Department said Carrie could go home, Dave took her back to his flat and insisted that she take his bed.

"I'll sleep on the couch," he said. "It's no problem."

"No," Carrie protested, though through her blocked-up nose it sounded more like, *Boh*. "I'll feel terrible turfing you out of your bed. I'm fine, honestly. I just need to rest for a bit."

The truth was, she ached all over from the attack, her head was full of cold and her throat was raw. If she didn't sit down soon, she was worried she would fall down.

"Carrie," Dave said in a 'patience in the face of gross stupidity' tone, "you look like death—"

"Thanks."

"So stop being an idiot and get into bed. Come in

here." He opened the door to the bedroom. "I changed the sheets this morning."

The room was predictably spick and span, and Dave had managed to make it look both stylish and extremely comfortable. Carrie sat down on the bed before her legs collapsed out from under her. Maybe she should rest, just for a while. "Thanks," she said sheepishly.

"Lie down and rest. The television remote is on that table next to the bed. I'll make some tea then pop out and get you some pyjamas and a change of clothes. You can't wear the same outfit forever, especially not after your attack. If I'm quick I can get to the shopping centre before it closes. Maybe try to get some sleep."

"But what's happening with the placktoids? And has Belinda sent any news?"

"You're in no condition to be dealing with this crisis right now, Carrie. But just to stop you from worrying, I can tell you that we closed off the factory after your attack. I informed Errruorerrrrrh about what happened, and we agreed to seal the remaining devices inside. There's clearly a connection between them and the placktoids, so to prevent the placktoids from opening a gateway inside and transporting them out, we're constructing a hollow steel shell over the whole thing, and the oootoon have agreed to send enough of themselves to fill it."

"That's so kind of them," said Carrie. The yellow, custard-like oootoon was the only known substance that gateways couldn't pass through. "I love those guys."

"Yes, well, they remember what you did for them and they were only too happy to help out. Oh, by the way, I asked Errruorerrrrh if she knew how you'd come to own Carrie Hatchett Enterprises, and she knew! She understood when I said we remembered a different past—that our time travel trip had triggered changes in the time line that everyone but us had lived. She said that in their time line, Gavin suspected there was a reason Apate went off with Bob from Accounts that night at the pub. Apparently, he told you to ask Bob about it, and Bob said Apate had pestered him with questions about the company and its products. She seemed to know a lot more about the company than she should, and Gavin thought it was very fishy. He recommended that the Council bought the company and put it under your control."

"And Matthias Cowper just sold it to me?" Carrie asked. "If he really is dandrobian, he must have known who I was."

"Maybe he arrogantly thought that when the invasion began and the products came alive, you would go down with the sinking ship."

"Maybe. Good old Gavin," Carrie said. "He's so clever. The Council are idiots for sacking him."

"You won't get any argument from me on that score," Dave replied. "Now, relax and concentrate on getting better." He went out and closed the door.

Carrie lay down. Dave was right, of course. She wasn't any use to anyone in her current state. As soon as her head touched the pillow, she felt her eyelids closing.

The next thing she knew, she was waking from a very deep sleep. Her body was stiff, as if she hadn't changed position while she was sleeping, but she guessed it was due to her numerous bruises and scrapes. New pyjamas and other clothes were still in their packets on the bedside table next to a box of tissues and a mug of tea.

Carrie sat up and touched the mug. It was cold. She looked out the window. It was just getting light outside. She'd slept all night. After blowing her nose thoroughly, she got up and went to find Dave.

The flat was empty, however. Dave had left a note on the coffee table.

> *Gone back to Scotland Yard. Eat whatever*
> *you want from the kitchen and get some*
> *rest. I'll probably be back late tonight.*
> *Don't wait up.*

Rogue was pushing his head against her hand, asking for a pat, and Toodles was winding herself around Carrie's legs. She gave her pets some reassuring cuddles before taking a shower.

While she'd been at the hospital, Carrie had been successful in avoiding looking at the results of the attack. As she put on her new pyjamas, however, she couldn't help but notice the bruises, cuts and scrapes that seemed to cover most of her body. If the Unity troops hadn't turned up when they did, things could have turned out a lot worse for her. Though her job with the Transgalactic Council came with risks, she didn't think she'd ever felt as much in danger as she had the previous evening in the factory.

Her new pyjamas covered up most of her injuries and while she was drying her hair, watching her reflection in Dave's full-length mirror, she noticed that they suited her very well too. The colour was flattering and they made her look taller and thinner.

"How does he *do* that?" she asked herself.

When Carrie returned to Dave's bedroom, Rogue and Toodles looked up at her guiltily from their position on top of the covers. Dave hadn't let them in the night before, but now that he was gone, they were trying their chances.

"I'm positive Dave won't approve, you two," Carrie said as she joined them on the bed and turned on the television. Before settling down to catch up on news about the placktoid invasion, however, Carrie went out to the kitchen. Her illness had dampened her appetite, but she'd remembered some cold cures she'd tried over the years.

It was the first time Carrie had seen the contents of Dave's kitchen. She realised that he had to love cooking. Inside his fridge and cupboards were all kinds of ingredients for making exotic dishes from scratch. Spices and herbs, sauces and condiments, oils, vinegars and other liquids, powders and granules, some of which she'd never seen before.

Carrie found a lemon and some honey and made herself a hot lemon drink. Then she boiled the kettle again and gathered dried chamomile, peppermint, sage, ginger, salt and pepper in a heatproof bowl. She also cut an onion into slices. When the water had boiled she poured it over the herbs and spices and grabbed a clean tea towel. Carrying the hot bowl, tea towel, lemon drink and onions on a tray, she went into the bedroom.

She found the previous day's socks and layered the onions inside the soles before putting them on. The onion slices were cold and damp to her feet, but she would soon get used to them, she decided. She tucked herself under the covers, set the bowl on her lap and put the tea towel over her head. While breathing in the aromatic steam, she listened to the morning news.

"Following an attack yesterday," the announcer was saying, "the manufacturing premises of Carrie Hatchett Enterprises have been put under round-the-clock armed guard."

Carrie lifted the tea towel and peeked out. The scene at the television studio cut to the street where her factory stood. It had been closed off and armed police stood at the barriers. Carrie guessed the ones in darkened visors were Unity troops. The factory itself was only visible in the distance. The police must have evacuated all the nearby premises.

The announcer's voice played over the visual of the street. "The rampaging robots crisis has deepened and still the authorities appear to have no explanation or solution. Requests for a press conference have been denied and the Metropolitan Police has not given an update for over six hours, except to state that earlier warnings still apply: All products manufactured by Carrie Hatchett Enterprises are subject to immediate recall. If you believe you may have bought a product from Carrie Hatchett Enterprises, contact this number." An 0800 number appeared at the bottom of the screen. "The Prime Minister remains missing. It is estimated that it is only a matter of hours before the government declares a State of Emergency."

***

Carrie had decided to return to the factory that had become a nest of baby devices. It was nighttime, and sleet was coming down hard. She didn't seem to really feel it much, though it was hard to see through it. The factory doors loomed ahead. The police tape had vanished and the Unity troops who were supposed to be guarding it seemed to be taking a break.

Carrie hadn't brought her key, but when she pushed on the door, it swung open. The factory was dark inside. Shadowy shapes were moving around. Placktoids. Baby ones scurried across the floor, moving as one, like a shoal of fish. The mechanical devices were dancing. They were performing a kind of ballet, leaping and pirouetting. Their movements were graceful and fluid. Behind them, like a menacing backdrop, the placktoids Carrie knew so well were standing.

All the familiar ones were there: massive paperclips like the very first of the mechanical aliens Carrie had met on the surface of Oootoon. It had whisked Dave and her away to their starship. There were the placktoids like giant Biros; metal staple removers; shredders with their towering rows of metal teeth; and, largest of all, a 3D printer like the one she had encountered on the placktoid's home planet millennia in the past.

Just as Carrie was wondering why none of the mechanical aliens seemed to have noticed her, and what she was even doing there anyway, alone and unprotected, the baby metal creatures froze and the ballet came to a halt. A device landed on one metal leg, breaking the sudden silence with a clang.

They had noticed her after all.

Carrie turned to the door, but it had swung shut silently behind her. She ran to open it, but it was locked. She faced the placktoids once more. In the split second she had turned away from them, they had advanced. The babies were first in line, inching along on their little caterpillar treads, wheels and levers. The adult devices were moving between them, drawing close to Carrie more quickly than their offspring. The placktoids bringing up the rear kept a steady pace.

Carrie felt around her person. She hadn't brought anything with her—no weapons, no translator, nothing that might help her fight off the aliens or subdue them. All she could find in her pockets was tissues. Hundreds and hundreds of tissues. Carrie began pulling them out in handfuls. She threw them at the placktoids, knowing the gesture was hopeless.

Her pockets were immediately full again. She took out more of the soft white tissues and tossed them forward. She was creating a blizzard of large, white snowflakes. She couldn't see the placktoids anymore through the descending cloud of paper. Had she defeated them?

One broke through the white storm. It was the 3D printer. Large and ominous, it towered over her.

"Would you like some tea?" it said.

"Wh-What?"

"I thought you might like some tea. Or do you need some more sleep?"

Sleep?

Carrie opened her eyes. Dave was standing over her holding a steaming mug. Rubbing her eyes, Carrie sat up. "I'd love some tea, thanks. I had the most awful dream. A nightmare, really. What's the time?"

"It's just gone one," he said. "You seem a bit better."

"I am feeling better. Having a long sleep helped. What's been happening? Any news? I thought you wouldn't be home until tonight."

He sat on the corner of the bed. "There isn't a lot to tell. The armed guard will stay at the factory while we figure out what we're dealing with."

"Wouldn't it be better to destroy the place?" Carrie asked. She gave a shudder as she recalled the hordes of small devices crawling over her and the larger ones beating her.

"We discussed that with the army, but it would be difficult to blow the place up without damaging the buildings around it. A big explosion would cause a fair amount of public alarm too. People are frightened enough as it is."

"Maybe it would be a bad idea for another reason," said Carrie. "Do you remember those baby placktoids we came across on their starship when we went to Oootoon? The ones I saw in my factory are the same kind of thing. The products my company was making can reproduce like organic life forms. It's like the ancient, undifferentiated placktoids we saw when we went back in time were the first type, then they evolved into the placktoids of today, and the ones my company made are the third type. A third-generation placktoid that can reproduce organically rather than having to manufacture new members.

"The placktoids might not be too pleased if we destroy their nest. Who knows what they might do? They already have the PM."

"That fits the facts," Dave said. "The question is, where do we go from here?"

"Still no word on the PM's whereabouts?"

"None at all. The Unity are scouring the placktoid planet for life signs, but it's a big place. They haven't found anything yet."

"If they don't find her soon, it'll be too late."

"I know, Carrie. Everyone knows."

"Sorry. Just thinking aloud."

Dave sniffed the air. "Can you smell..." He sniffed again. "Onions? And what's in this bowl?" He was looking at the herb and spice steam infusion, which had become cold and looked like dirty dish water.

"Oh," said Carrie, pulling her feet from under the covers. "I've been trying some cold cures." She showed him her bulky footwear.

"You've got onions in your socks?"

"Yes. There's a theory that—"

"Onions in your socks. In my bed."

"Yes. About that..."

Dave held up a hand. "I don't want to hear it." He stood and went to the door. "If you're feeling better, you can get up and come back with me to London. The Commissioner is renting a flat for us so we don't have to commute every day. The landlord accepts pets."

CHAPTER THIRTEEN

Their new, temporary home was in a small block of flats not far from Scotland Yard. It was a modest place, though it must have cost thousands a month to rent. While Carrie was helping Toodles and Rogue feel at home, Dave was talking on the phone.

When the call ended, he said, "I'm going back to the Met's headquarters. Some reports of suspected sightings of placktoids in other areas of Europe and Africa came in while we were driving down."

"Do you think they're to be believed?"

"It wouldn't be hard for placktoids to sneak aboard container ships, so yes, I think there's a good chance they're spreading over the globe. That seems to be their plan."

"First Earth, then the galaxy." Carrie tried to remember if her company exported overseas. Maybe the third-generation placktoids were in other countries too.

"I have to go," Dave said. "Are you going to be okay?"

"Yes," Carrie replied, though she noticed the horrible, clogged up, headachey feeling of her cold returning a while ago. "I'll be fine. Don't worry about me. I had an idea about a lead, in fact. We haven't been able to locate the placktoids, but we might be able to find their accomplices. As far as I could tell the person who started up my company, Matthias Cowper, is still working for the BBC. I'm going to go there and talk to him."

"Are you positive he's dandrobian? I looked up his records and everything checks out. Birth certificate, vaccinations, school registration, exams he took, the lot. I see what you mean about his looks, but apart from that..."

"He is dandrobian, Dave. I just know it. Those records must be faked. You know how clever they are."

"I'll speak to the Commissioner, then. He can authorise a police officer to accompany you."

"No. I'd rather not put Mr. Cowper on his guard. He might give more away if it's just me who sees him."

"All right. It's up to you. But be careful. You don't want a repeat of what happened to you at the factory."

"I will."

After Dave had left, Carrie took a bulb of garlic out of her jacket pocket. She'd brought them from Dave's flat. She was sure she'd read somewhere that chewing raw garlic for thirty seconds then spitting it out would make her symptoms go away. It was worth a try.

She broke off some cloves, removed the skin and chewed them. The taste was sharp and strong and by the time she spat them into the kitchen bin, her mouth was numb. Still, they did seem to do the trick. Her nose was clear and her throat felt better, though she wasn't sure if it was only numb like her mouth.

Carrie made sure Rogue and Toodles had plenty of water and toys to play with before she set off into the cold outdoors. She took the Tube to Broadcasting House. She wasn't sure how she was going to get inside the headquarters of the BBC to speak to Matthias Cowper, but she was sure she would think of something on the way.

For some reason, the other passengers on the Tube trains gave her a wide berth. Considering it was rush hour and the train was packed, it was very strange. She wondered if she still looked as though she had a bad cold.

When she arrived at Broadcasting House, she went into the reception area. The nasty virus that had caused her cold appeared to be spreading. Another visitor to the BBC clapped his hand over his nose and face when she drew near. He scurried away. Carrie went up to the receptionist. "I'm here to see Matthias Cowper."

The man tapped Cowper's name into a keyboard and scanned the results that appeared on his screen. "Mr. Cowper doesn't have any appointments today." The man raised an eyebrow, then something seemed to hit him. Like the person Carrie had passed on her way in, he grabbed his nose. She marvelled at the virulence of the cold she'd caught. It was going through the population like wildfire.

Though, in fact, the receptionist looked as though he was about to vomit. Maybe he had a tummy bug.

"I don't have an appointment," said Carrie, "but I must speak to Mr. Cowper. It's very important."

"I'm sorry, but he's busy. Perhaps you can make an appointment and come back another day."

"I don't have time to come back. I have to see him now." Carrie folded her arms and leaned on the reception desk. She glared at the receptionist. "I'm not moving from this spot until he comes out to speak to me."

The man swallowed. He had turned green. Carrie felt a little sorry for him, but if he was ill he should have stayed home.

Scowling, the receptionist picked up his phone and punched an extension number into his keypad. He held his hand over the mouthpiece as he muttered into the phone. Carrie couldn't make out what he was saying. After a few moments' urgent conversation, he hung up. "Mr. Cowper will be out to see you in a moment. You can wait over there." He pointed to the seats on the other side of the reception area.

"Thanks," said Carrie as she went to sit down.

The receptionist took out a can of air freshener and sprayed it all around him.

CHAPTER FOURTEEN

Matthias Cowper looked exactly like the photograph Carrie had seen on the internet, though it had been taken several years previously. His lack of aging wasn't surprising—dandrobians were immortal.

The BBC assistant producer walked over to Carrie, his hand outstretched, smiling as though she were a long-lost friend. Another typical dandrobian habit. They were extremely charming, but Carrie was used to their ways. She'd fallen victim to them before. She wasn't going to let it happen a second time.

"Mr. Cowper," she said, standing as he approached. "Thanks for agreeing to speak to me at short notice."

"Oh, er..." Matthias Cowper's smile faded as he drew close enough to shake hands. Dropping hers like a hot coal, he backed away. "Let me get you some coffee."

"It's okay. I don't drink coffee."

"Tea, then."

"No, thanks." In fact, after staying at Dave's, Carrie had drunk enough tea to last a lifetime. Brewing the beverage seemed to be Dave's main occupation when he was at home.

"Water?" Mr. Cowper's voice was tight, as if he was stressed about something, which Carrie found highly suspicious. Had he guessed why she was there? The receptionist hadn't asked her name, so she didn't think he would have made the connection yet.

"No."

"Juice?"

"I'm really not thirsty, thank you," Carrie replied, mildly irritated. The man seemed obsessed with liquids. It was odd. She recalled the delicious nectar she'd drunk on Dandrobia. She was sure nothing on Earth matched up to it. She wondered if he missed his home planet. Also, she mused, what was his real name? Was he also a minor Greek god like the two dandrobians she'd unwittingly allowed to escape their confinement on Dandrobia?

Matthias Cowper apparently needed plenty of physical space. He kept himself a good distance from Carrie as he led her towards an entrance to the inner offices staffed by a security guard. The man took Carrie's details and gave her a security pass on a lanyard to wear. Cowper escorted her through the entrance and into the BBC.

In spite of the seriousness of her mission there, Carrie couldn't help but feel a small thrill of excitement as she went in. She'd never been behind the scenes of a television company before. She was intrigued about what happened there. Would she meet someone famous?

"It's very flattering that you should ask to see me," Cowper said. "Assistant producers rarely attract much attention. But I'm afraid we don't have any internships available at the moment in my department. I'll take you to HR where you can talk to someone about other opportunities at the BBC. I assume you've brought your CV?"

"What? No," Carrie exclaimed. "I'm not here for a job. Is that what you thought?"

"Oh." Cowper halted and turned to her. "That is what I assumed. That's the usual reason for impromptu visits. Did you wish to discuss something else? I'd be happy to talk to you about any of the documentaries I've worked on, but you really will have to make an appointment and come back. Or perhaps we could speak over the phone. I'm afraid I'm rather busy today."

"I'm not here for any of those reasons, Mr. Cowper. Perhaps if I told you my name? You didn't listen when I told the security guard, did you? I'm Carrie Hatchett."

Though it lasted less than a second, a look of shock registered on Cowper's face before he managed to quickly suppress it. He smiled once more, though more stiffly. "Carrie Hatchett? The name does seem familiar, though I don't believe I've had the honour of your acquaintance."

These dandrobians, Carrie thought. They were arch-beguilers. If only they used their powers for good, the galaxy would be a better place.

"It's no use lying to me, Cowper," said Carrie. "If that's even your real name. I have it in black and white that you set up my company, currently called Carrie Hatchett Enterprises. I've guessed a lot more about you than you might think."

"Of course," Cowper said, his expression not flickering for a moment. "Carrie Hatchett Enterprises. That little business I set up. Such an unfortunate turn of events. Was it turning a handsome profit before the crisis? You have some funds salted away somewhere I hope? But wait. Before you answer, let's find somewhere more private to chat, shall we?"

"We can do this here or wherever you choose," said Carrie. "The outcome will be the same."

In truth, she wasn't at all sure exactly what she expected to get out of Cowper. The entire story of the dandrobian involvement with the placktoids and their plan to take over the galaxy would have been ideal, but she doubted the alien would give away anything if he could avoid it. Bluffing probably wouldn't hurt, however.

The dandrobian raised his eyebrows at her words. "How very dramatic. I'm intrigued at what you believe this outcome to be. Do come with me."

He led her deeper into the building. Disappointingly, the interior of Broadcasting House didn't look much different from ordinary offices. For a long-standing broadcasting company of world renown, the place looked rather boring.

Cowper knocked on a door. When no one answered, he opened it. After peeking in, he opened the door wider and gestured to Carrie to go inside. The room was small and apparently intended for interviews or meetings. She went around a table and sat down.

"Would you mind waiting here for just a moment?" Cowper asked. "I need a coffee if you don't." Before Carrie could answer, he went out quickly, closing the door.

Carrie went after him, but when she opened the door and looked into the corridor, he had disappeared. She returned to the room. It was possible that Cowper was making a quick exit, but she thought it was unlikely. He was probably as interested to find out what she knew or had guessed as she was for him to answer her questions. Even if the dandrobian decided to make a run for it, Carrie had the manpower and skills of the Metropolitan Police at her disposal. Matthias Cowper was highly noticeable. He wouldn't get far.

Cowper returned, minus the coffee he'd said he was getting. He sat opposite Carrie and relaxed into his chair, smiling at her effortlessly. "I confess I'm dying to know why you're here, Carrie Hatchett. Please begin."

He was putting the ball in her court, hoping to draw something important from her. "It's obvious why I'm here, Cowper. It's you who has to explain yourself. You know it's the products made by Carrie Hatchett Enterprises that are currently running amok and terrorising the innocent citizens of Britain, and perhaps soon the world. What did you do when you set up the manufacture of those devices? What is it about them that makes them behave as they do?"

Cowper affected a look of great concern. "I would love to help you, darling. Really, I would. But I'm afraid I have simply no idea *what* you're talking about."

His demeanor spoke of complete confusion and innocence. At one time, Carrie might have believed him. His performance was utterly convincing. Before her stint on Dandrobia, she might have been taken in. But that was a different Carrie.

She leaned forward and looked into Cowper's gorgeous brown eyes. He covered his nose and leaned backward.

"You old ham," Carrie said. "You don't...ah." Her nose was tickling her again. She fought the urge to sneeze. "You don't...ah...ah...fool..." Her eyes watered. The garlic she'd chewed was wearing off. The symptoms of her cold were returning in full force. "You...don't...ah...ah...atchoo!"

Carrie's sneeze caused the dandrobian to leap up in disgust, knocking over his chair. "Well, really," he exclaimed. He pulled a cloth handkerchief out of his pocket and wiped his face.

At the same time, the door opened and two women and a man entered. They were all tall, perfectly proportioned and beautiful. More dandrobians. More dandrobians than just Matthias Cowper were working at the BBC. They must have escaped from Dandrobia too.

"Outrageous behaviour," said one of the female

dandrobians, though none of them had witnessed Carrie's sneeze. They'd arrived a second too late. Carrie had done nothing outrageous in front of her.

"I agree," said the other. "We must call security."

"I'll do it," said the male dandrobian. He keyed a number into his phone and spoke into it. "We have an extremely disruptive visitor in room seven-oh-nine. Could we please have a security detail to escort her from the building?"

Carrie was about to protest but another massive sneeze was building. She grabbed the packet of tissues in her pocket. "I don't...ah...I didn't...ah..."

Cowper and the other dandrobians watched her smugly as they waited for the building's security officers to arrive. They had set her up.

"Atchoo!"

Carrie blew her nose and gave a great, hacking cough.

Two security officers came into the room.

"This woman is over-excited and disturbed," Cowper said. "Please show her the exit."

"Ah yes," an officer replied. "Reception told us about her. Come with us, madam. It'll be better for everyone if you leave now."

"Atchoo!"

CHAPTER FIFTEEN

By the time Dave returned that evening, Carrie had drunk two shots of whiskey mixed with peppermint schnapps and apple cider vinegar. She'd added some cinnamon and honey for good measure and rubbed both camphor and Vicks on her chest. None of her remedies had made the symptoms of her cold go away, but she at least didn't care about them anymore.

She was lying on the sofa, nursing her empty glass and wondering if she should have another dose of the new medicinal cocktail she'd invented when Dave came in from the hall. She lifted a hand and was about to greet her friend, but she sneezed instead.

"Bother this damned cold," she said and gave a sniff as she searched for a tissue.

"Are you looking for these?" Dave asked. He handed her the tissue packet that was sitting on her lap. How had she missed it?

"Thanks," Carrie said before blowing her nose.

"What have you been drinking? And what's that smell?"

"Just some of this." Carrie picked up the open whiskey bottle she'd put on the floor next to the sofa. "And a little bit of that." She pointed at the schnapps bottle on Dave's bookshelf. "And I put in a teaspoon of cinnamon. I bought some on the way home. It's a c—"

"Cold cure," interrupted Dave. "Yes. I guessed. Don't you think you'd be better off in bed with some hot lemon and honey?"

"I tried that. And I tried breathing in steam that was infu...infu...infu...mixed with herbs. And I tried...oh, I forget." She sat up, feeling surprisingly dizzy. Perhaps a second medicinal cocktail wasn't such a good idea. "Dave, what are we going to do? I tried to get some information from Matthias Cowper today and he had me thrown out. I was thrown out of Broadcasting House for causing a disturbance."

"You were causing a disturbance?"

"No, of course I wasn't. There were more dandrobians there. They've infiltrated the place. They lied and told the security guards I was crazy."

"Was that before or after you'd been drinking whiskey and peppermint schnapps?"

Carrie rolled her eyes. "Before. The point is, I didn't find out anything. All I did was let them know that we're onto them. They'll be even more cautious not to let anything slip now. I wasted my chance. It's this cold. I can't think straight." She gasped. "They must have

106

escaped from Dandrobia years ago, around the time my company was set up. They must have snuck or bribed their way through a gateway like Apate and Notos did. I bet they set up gateways like the one on the train. Placktoids must have been pouring in through them. If only I could have made Cowper tell me something. I've screwed up."

Dave picked up the two bottles of alcohol and put on the lids. "You're being a bit hard on yourself. Did you really think Matthias Cowper was going to give anything away? You know how intelligent dandrobians are."

"I do know. So why did I go there and alert them to the fact that we're on to them? Why not ask the Commissioner to bring him in for questioning?"

"I don't think the police can interrogate whoever they choose. They have to have a good reason. And Cowper's background checked out. The others' would have too, I'm sure."

"You mean that setting up a company that manufactured machines that come to life and attack their owners isn't a good reason for the police to interview someone?" Carrie asked.

"You've got a point. I'll call the Commissioner. He gave me his direct number."

While they were waiting for the head of the Metropolitan Police to answer, Carrie asked, "Anything happen today?"

Dave shook his head. "The placktoids are still lying low. I think they're preparing for a massive campaign to take over the planet. Then they'll use Earth as their base from which they'll invade the rest of the galaxy." He spoke into his mobile. "Hello? It's Dave, sir. Carrie and I might have a lead. Someone by the name of Matthias Cowper started Carrie Hatchett Enterprises. Do you agree it would be a good idea to talk to him?" He listened.

"Really?" he went on. "Carrie found his name on the computer records at her offices. There's no doubt in our minds he's the original owner." He listened some more. "Great. Could you let us know when you have him?" He ended the call.

"There's a good reason the police didn't investigate Matthias Cowper," Dave said. "It turns out, according to the records at Companies' House, the original owner is you."

"The records state that *I'm* the founder of the company?"

"Yeah. The dandrobians must have found a way to tamper with the records. Only they didn't or couldn't access the company's own records to change them after you took over."

"So if I hadn't gone into the office to check them, we wouldn't have known about Matthias Cowper?"

"That's right. See. You aren't as stupid as you look." Dave smirked.

Carrie threw a cushion at his head, though she was also smiling. Then her smile faded. "This isn't a time for joking. We have to find the poor Prime Minister or persuade the placktoids to return her."

"Yeah. Maybe Matthias Cowper will give us a clue, or

maybe Belinda will turn up something."

"You haven't heard from her?"

"No. Not since she left."

"Maybe she's gone over to the dandrobians?" Carrie's eyes widened. "What if she's told them everything?"

"Carrie. Stop it."

"Well, you never know." She blew her nose. "Drat this cold."

"Maybe some tea will help?"

"Er, thanks, but I think I've had enough—"

"Lemon tea?"

Carrie sighed. "Go on, then."

"I'll make us some dinner too. We should have time to eat before the police bring in Matthias Cowper. Then I'll head back to take part in the interview."

"You've been holding the fort like a champ, Dave. I feel so bad letting you do everything."

"Huh, says the person who discovered the placktoid nest and the dandrobian infiltration."

"Oh." Carrie's mouth fell open as a thought struck her.

Dave paused in the hall. "What?"

"The placktoid nest. What's happening with that?"

"Nothing's changed as far as I know. The police have the area cordoned off and the army and Unity are guarding the place. Why?"

"I can't believe it. We've been total idiots. Dave, what would you do if someone had your family under lock and key?"

"What do you mean?"

"What would you do if someone had kidnapped your family. What would you be prepared to do to free them?"

"Anything, of course. I'd do anything to save my family."

"Exactly. We've been holding a trump card all this time without realising it. We've been worried about the third generation placktoids escaping, or the others breaking in to rescue them. We haven't been thinking about how we could use them."

"Use them? How can we use them? We can't control them."

"I mean use them as a bargaining tool. The placktoids might have our Prime Minister, but we have their babies. Their *babies*, Dave."

"Wow." He returned to the living room and closed the door. "I never thought of it like that. But, I don't know. On the placktoid starship, they just abandoned the baby paperclips. Maybe they don't feel the same about their offspring as we do."

"There's one way we can find out," said Carrie. "Why don't we threaten to do something dire to the little buggers if they don't return the Prime Minister immediately?"

"Something dire? Like what?" Dave's phone rang. He looked at the screen and said, "It's the Commissioner," before answering. "Hello? Yes. Okay. I'll be over there in ten minutes. I want to speak to you about something else first. Carrie has an idea."

CHAPTER SIXTEEN

The question was, how were they supposed to get a message to the placktoids when no one knew where they were or how to reach them? Carrie and Dave had gone to the Commissioner's office to draft a statement. While she was composing the message with Dave, Carrie was listening in to the Commissioner's phone conversation with his technical team.

"I see. How long will that take to set up?" the Commissioner asked. "Right. Please arrange it as quickly as you can and let me know when it's ready. We'll broadcast immediately." He hung up and turned to Carrie and Dave. "How is that statement coming along?"

"Nearly done," Dave replied, frowning as he typed the closing sentence. "What do you think, Carrie?"

She read the whole message through again, including the part Dave had just added. "I like it. I think we're being more than reasonable in the circumstances. If they don't agree to this, they'll only have themselves to blame for what happens next. Do we have an ETA on the Unity starships?"

Dave replied, "Errruorerrrrrh said tomorrow morning."

"So how long do you think we should give the placktoids to comply?"

"I would advise not giving them very long," said the Commissioner. "A drawn-out negotiation isn't to our advantage in this scenario. We'll be putting the placktoids under a direct threat, and the longer they have to give an answer, the more opportunity they have to organise a strong, decisive response. I would advise two hours as a maximum."

"Two hours is plenty of time to do as we demand," said Carrie. "They have gateways."

"Right," Dave said. "But how can we be sure they'll even get the message?"

The Commissioner answered, "We're going to broadcast the message on all television channels and radio stations simultaneously. My team said they can arrange it. The placktoids won't fail to see the statement. The method isn't ideal. I would prefer that the general public were not aware of what we're doing. I don't want to cause any panic. However, I believe we have to risk some alarm at this stage. We have the permission of the Deputy Prime Minister, who is informing the heads of the armed services as we speak so they can prepare to respond to incidences of civil unrest. I assume you've left out any references to aliens or planets in your message, as we discussed?"

Carrie nodded. What they were about to do might be the turning point in the plactoid invasion. She only hoped that their plan would work. They had Errruorerrrrrhch's approval, which added to her confidence.

The Commissioner's telephone rang. He answered it. "All set? Good. We'll come down."

The three of them went downstairs to the room reserved for press conferences. As they went into the room, the Commissioner said, "Which one of you is going to read the statement?"

"I thought you were going to read it," said Carrie.

"As I understand it," said the Inspector, "the plactoids are familiar with both of you. I believe they may be more willing to comply when they're faced with individuals who have defeated them in the past. If the statement is read by one of you, it may have more impact."

"Hmmm," said Carrie. "It might also make them more likely to want to defy us. The bad blood between Dave and I and the plactoids stretches back a long way."

"I still believe it would be better if one of you were to read it."

Carrie turned to Dave. "Looks like it's down to you. I won't sound convincing with my nose stuffed up and I can't guarantee I won't sneeze right in the middle of speaking."

"Two good points," Dave said. "All right. I'll do it."

The reporters and photographers were still filing into the press room, after being given only short notice. Carrie couldn't help but feel uncomfortable in the media representatives' presence, due to her encounter with them when the news of her company's involvement in the crisis broke.

"Actually," she said to Dave. "There's no reason for me to even join you on the podium, is there? I'd rather not. I've had enough publicity to last a lifetime."

"Fair enough," Dave replied. "I'm sure I'll manage."

"Can I borrow your phone?" Carrie asked.

"Sure." He handed it over.

After explaining to the Commissioner that she was going to remain on the sidelines during the reading of the statement, Carrie hung back while he and Dave went to the podium in the centre of the room. She opened the BBC News live stream on Dave's phone to watch the event as the public would see it.

A couple of reporters called out questions before the Commissioner and Dave had even reached the podium. "What's the latest on the Prime Minister?" one asked. "Has a body been found?"

Urgh, Carrie thought. The press were circling like vultures, hoping to be the first to report bad news.

On the screen of Dave's mobile, a report about a football game was playing. Then the broadcast switched to the news studio, and the word 'newsflash' ran across the bottom of the screen . A news presenter was straightening her jacket. She paused a moment, waiting for the autocue to play.

"We interrupt the scheduled report to bring you news of a development in the rampaging robots crisis. The Commissioner of the Metropolitan Police and a Government adviser have called a press conference. We're informed that they are about to read a statement to the head of the robot army. Switching to the press conference now."

The screen blinked, and Carrie saw the room through the lens of a camera facing the podium. The Commissioner seemed smaller on television than in real life. Dave was predictably photogenic.

The Commissioner briefly thanked the media representatives for coming. Many were still hurrying into the room and taking seats. Then he stepped back and Dave moved forward, the hastily printed statement in his hands.

"I speak on behalf of Her Majesty's Government and the people of Britain," Dave said. "This is a message to the leader of the mechanical beings who are attempting to take over our country.

"We have in our possession certain items very precious to you. If you refuse to comply with our requests, we will transport those precious objects of yours to a far distant, secret location and you will never find them again. We demand that you return our Prime Minister and that you vacate this country and return to your home, where you will live in confinement indefinitely. You have two hours to comply.

"We know who you are, and we know what you

want. You will not succeed. We have defeated you in the past and we shall do so again."

After reading out the final sentence, Dave looked directly into the camera. Carrie shivered. If he wanted to, Dave could look really mean.

Cameras had been clicking as Dave spoke. As soon as he finished speaking, the assembled reporters leapt up and began shouting out questions, ignoring attempts by the Commissioner to quieten them.

On her friend's mobile, the screen switched back to the BBC News presenter, who offered comments on the statement. Carrie couldn't hear what she was saying over the noise of the chaotic scene in the press room.

The BBC presenter had only been speaking a minute or so, however, when the scene changed again. A massive placktoid took up the whole screen. Its screeching was barely audible over the ruckus of the press reporters. Carrie lifted the phone to her ear.

The placktoid leader was laughing loudly. Carrie winced and held the phone a few inches away from her head. The terrible screeching stopped, and the placktoid began to speak. Carrie brought the mobile closer and concentrated on the sound.

"Foolish humans. You have already lost the battle for your planet, only you do not realise it. People of Britain, your Prime Minister lives, though barely. Soon, she will die, yet it will not be sufficient revenge for the destruction of so many of our fallen cousins' lives. You will pay, over and over, for what you have done. And when we have succeeded in seizing control, and your lives are nothing but terrible, agonised burdens to you, perhaps we will listen to your pleadings for release and grant your wishes.

"Until then, watch and suffer. Soon, you will grieve for the happy, carefree lives you once knew while you monstrously enslaved our kind."

CHAPTER SEVENTEEN

Carrie hardly recognised the old, Victorian factory that belonged to Carrie Hatchett Enterprises. A steel shell covered it top to bottom and over the roof. The result was a building-sized metal box. Though nothing was visible from the outside, within the double-walled shell was the layer of oootoon that prevented the placktoids from entering or leaving the place via transgalactic gateway.

The plan was to go inside and leave the doors open so that the Council could create their own gateway. Then, the Unity troops would force the third-generation placktoids through to a secret planet before they could be rescued. The supporting units of police, army and air force, who were providing helicopter support, had all been briefed.

Carrie and Dave were present in an advisory capacity due to their experience and expertise, but Carrie had insisted that she was also to enter the factory when it was opened. The bruises, cuts and grazes the third-gen placktoids had inflicted upon her had begun to heal, but she would feel a lot better when she saw the last of the devices, including the little ones, disappear through a gateway portal.

She was wearing a Liaison Officer uniform that Errruorerrrrrhch had sent through to replace the one lost when her house was destroyed. The uniform would signal to any placktoids surreptitiously observing the proceedings that she would be acting in her capacity as a representative of the Transgalactic Council. It also kept out the cold very well. The ground was slick with ice and a winter wind was gusting, swirling with flecks of snow.

"Are you sure you're up to this?" asked Dave.

Carrie was blowing her nose, which was red and sore from it being blown so much. "Yes. I'm okay. It's the third day of this cold. I should be feeling better soon." The truth was, she didn't feel at all better. But cold or no, witnessing the departure of the third-gen placktoids would brighten her day.

That was, of course, assuming that the placktoids weren't going to agree to their demands. From the tone of the leader's reply to their message, it seemed safe to conclude that they wouldn't.

"Don't you think it's a bit sad that the placktoids don't care about what happens to their babies?" Carrie asked Dave.

"Yes, it is. Though to be honest I'm not surprised.

They are made of metal after all."

"But the third generation aren't, or not entirely, and from what I saw when I went inside the factory, they do care about their little ones. They'd built a special area for them, like they were trying to protect them."

"Well it's a shame for us that their creators don't feel the same way. The baby plactoids could have been a great bargaining tool otherwise. Looks like we're back to square one. Again."

Carrie nodded glumly. "Still, I think we're right to carry out our threat anyway. If we didn't they'd think we're weak and they'd never pay any attention to us ever again."

Dave was checking his phone. "Five minutes."

"Who's giving the signal?" Carrie asked.

"Deputy PM," Dave replied. "By telephone."

The Deputy Prime Minister had been under armed guard at his residence ever since the beginning of the crisis. Losing the Prime Minister was unfortunate. Losing both the Prime Minister and the Deputy PM would only be viewed as grossly incompetent.

Two soldiers stood at the sealed steel double doors at the front of the factory, waiting for the order to unlock them. A platoon of more soldiers was lined up, waiting. In front of them stood Unity troops carrying their anti-plactoid weapons.

"How have the Unity soldiers been getting along?" Carrie asked Dave.

"They seem fine'" he replied. "I had some unusual requests, though. One of them only eats mollusc shells, and another one requested a freezer to sleep in." He was watching his phone as he spoke. "Three minutes."

Carrie blew her nose again. If she was at home, she would have stuffed a tissue up each nostril and have done with it. Such behaviour probably wouldn't do much for her image out there in public. Overhead, a blanket of dark grey cloud moved swiftly across the sky, covering it. Icy sleet began to fall. Carrie stamped her feet. The waiting was becoming unbearable.

Dave said, "One minute."

Carrie looked over her shoulder at the Commissioner, who was holding a mobile to his ear. He was also watching the door.

The seconds counted down to zero. The Commissioner nodded to the army officer, who gave a signal to his soldiers. The double doors were unlocked and flung wide, and the Unity soldiers ran inside. The British soldiers sped after them.

Carrie went forward. She wouldn't be doing any fighting. The Unity troops and soldiers were better at that than her. But she would be there to request from Errruorerrrrrhch the opening of the gateway and supervise the ushering through of the third-gen placktoids. Their intended destination was so top secret, even she didn't know where they were being sent. The governments of Earth and the Transgalactic Council hadn't given up hope that they might be a bargaining pawn in the future.

She peered into the dark interior of the factory. Sealing the place in a gateway-proof shell meant the electricity supply remained cut off, but the soldiers carried torches. The troops were carrying out a methodical search of the place.

The shelves nearest the front door, where Carrie had first spotted the third-gen placktoids were empty except for cardboard boxes. The machines must have relocated during their confinement. She glanced behind her, momentarily worried that they might slip out the open door behind her. But two Unity troops stood at the entrance, their weapons trained, to prevent escapes.

Where had the mechanical beings gone? Carrie had Dave's translator/communicator to request a gateway as soon as the devices were located. She held the device to her lips, ready to make the request. The soldiers were taking a long time to locate the prisoners.

Someone cursed loudly. Carrie spun around. The placktoids had been found at last. She was about to request the gateway, but the soldier finished his utterance with, "I nearly fell in."

Carrie went over to the shadowy figure near the middle of the room who had spoken.

The commanding officer also approached. The soldier squatted down and shined his torch at the floor. However, rather than forming a pool of light as Carrie would have expected, the light from the soldier's torch disappeared. Her heart began to sink as realisation set in.

The commanding officer also cursed. He spoke into his radio, ordering his platoon to stop searching.

A moment later, Carrie arrived at the spot. It was as she'd feared. At the center of the factory, between the manufacturing equipment and the packing area, was a large hole. Even in the light of the soldier's torch, she couldn't see its base.

Of course they hadn't been able to find any third-generation placktoids. Encasing the factory in oootoon hadn't been enough. Placktoids were machines and they could dig. The mechanical aliens had outwitted them again, finding an obvious method of escape. In the light of the soldier's torch, the tunnel that led away from the factory wasn't visible, but it had to be there. The third-generation placktoids were long gone. No wonder their leader had laughed when it heard their threat.

Carrie had reached the end of her tether. She was ill, exhausted and out of ideas. Her hopes that she or anyone else might foil the plans of the evil mechanical aliens finally foundered. The placktoids had escaped their time shield, they had somehow triggered the awakening of the third-generation of their kind, they had kidnapped Britain's PM, and their dandrobian accomplices had been living in Britain for years, preparing for their invasion.

Carrie's and Dave's efforts, along with those of the best of the British police and defence forces, had failed. If they didn't do something right soon, humanity and the rest of the galaxy would be living under the control of the placktoids.

CHAPTER EIGHTEEN

Belinda was back. Dave had asked the half-dandrobian to come to the flat to tell them what she'd discovered. It was past midnight and both he and Carrie were out of energy and ideas. They also had to bring Belinda up to date on what had been happening on Earth.

It was that part of the impending conversation that Carrie was dreading. Belinda was kind of all right, some of the time, Carrie supposed, but she just couldn't resist pointing out everyone else's mistakes.

"I'll make some tea," Dave said before leaving Carrie and Belinda alone in his living room. The statuesque half-dandrobian was taking up most of the space on the sofa, so Carrie had retreated to the armchair. Rogue was resting his head on her knee, and Toodles, after hissing her dislike of Belinda, had stalked from the room in a huff.

The reversal in the cat's attitude to dandrobians—

even half-dandrobians—was one of the things Carrie appreciated most about the tweaks to the time line caused by her and Dave's trips into the past.

"I take it things didn't go too well while I was away?" Belinda asked. "Have you found where the placktoids are hiding? Any news on the PM?"

Carrie replied, "We'd better wait until Dave gets back with the tea. Then we can tell you everything."

"I heard about the escape of the one bargaining tool we had," Belinda went on regardless. Her eyes were on Carrie. In spite of the actual words she spoke, what Carrie heard from Belinda was, *You let the one bargaining tool we had escape.*

Carrie gritted her teeth and looked expectantly at the door. "He's taking a long time with that tea, isn't he?"

"And I heard that dandrobians have been hiding out at the BBC. What happened there? I heard you—"

Carrie exclaimed, "I did not—"

"Here we are," Dave said as he came in carrying a tray of mugs and a bowl of sugar.

"Great," Carrie said. "Thanks." She took a mug from the tray. "Maybe you should go first, Belinda. I'm dying to hear what you found out on Dandrobia."

"Quite a lot, actually," she said, smirking. She tossed back her hair. "Honestly, I'm a little ashamed to be related to my father's people. For all their skills in genetically engineering themselves, they don't seem to have bothered eradicating their worst traits: vanity and arrogance. I'm so glad I take after my mother."

Carrie inwardly rolled her eyes.

Belinda continued, "I didn't have to do much flattering or eavesdropping to hear about their friends the placktoids and references to how, when they called in their favours, things would be like they were in the good old days."

"Favours?" Dave asked.

"Yes," Belinda replied, "it took me a while to figure it out from piecing together comments and hints I heard here and there, but in the end I figured out that the biggest favour was enabling the placktoids to circumvent the time shield the Council put down to seal them in their past." She took a sip of tea. "It was very simple, really. Though the placktoids were trapped in time, they weren't trapped at their planet. They still had gateway technology, even if the temporal aspect wouldn't work. The placktoids simply went to Dandrobia."

"The Dandrobia of the past?" asked Carrie.

"Exactly. At that time, the dandrobians had only recently been confined to their planet. Imagine their surprise when mechanical aliens suddenly turned up—mechanical aliens from the future, who told them that in return for their help, they would eventually free them from their prison and share control of the galaxy with them."

"Whoa," Dave exclaimed. "So when did the placktoids first become involved with the dandrobians?"

"I wondered that too," said Belinda. "From what I

overheard, I couldn't tell. Dandrobians experience time differently from us due to their immortality. They talk about things that happened to them in the distant past like it was yesterday."

"But it's possible that the time shield was actually the catalyst for the placktoids teaming up with the dandrobians?" Carrie asked.

"As I understand it, yes," Belinda replied. "Gavin would have more to say about the time paradox implications. It doesn't really matter anyway. What's done is done. What matters is that the placktoids did persuade the dandrobians to help them. And now we have two enemies to face. It won't be long before my father's people make their move. They've been developing weapons in those secret underground technology centres. All they needed was a powerful ally at their side. Now they have the placktoids."

"But if the dandrobians had access to gateway technology all these years, why didn't they just use it to escape from their planet?" Dave asked. "Why did they wait to use the squashpump negotiation crisis as a ruse to escape through Carrie's gateway?"

"The Council is monitoring Dandrobia for gateways leaving the planet, remember?" said Belinda. "That was why the two dandrobians whom Carrie allowed to escape had to use a gateway she had requested. They couldn't use one of their own or the Council would have spotted it."

"So the placktoids couldn't leave the planet even though they had the technology to do it," said Dave.

"But wait, there were placktoids on the squashpump planet at that time too. How was that possible if they were all trapped on Dandrobia?"

Carrie was mulling over the 'whom Carrie allowed to escape' part of Belinda's sentence.

"You're assuming they all went to the past," Belinda replied. "I think it's obvious from that fact that they didn't. Anyway, when Carrie allowed the dandrobians to come here, they tampered with her gateway portal and created the other on the train. They must have developed the technology to make the gateways that arrive at those portals undetectable. I'd also guess that if these persons at the BBC really are dandrobians who sneaked off Dandrobia in a similar way, then they also created portals here, and placktoids have flooded onto Earth. Now both groups are simply waiting for the right time to strike."

Carrie's head was hurting, and it wasn't only due to her cold. She was trying to figure out the time line. After the placktoids were defeated on the water planet where she'd undergone basic training, they'd gone into the past to try to change the course of history. Then Dave and she had followed them back in time and defeated their plans again. After that, because they couldn't move into the future, they went sideways and travelled to Dandrobia.

"So," Carrie said as an incredulous realisation settled in, "you mean to say the placktoids have been on Dandrobia all this time? Millennia? Just waiting for their chance?"

Belinda turned her amber eyes to Carrie's. "Yes. Some of them at least. I think the dandrobians must have placed them in some kind of suspended animation to prevent them from deteriorating. But it's worse than that. I'm almost certain that the reason Earth was chosen as the springboard for their attack on the rest of the galaxy is because of you."

Carrie detected an accusatory tone to Belinda's words. She folded her arms. "I know I'm not perfect, Belinda, as you're so fond of pointing out. But now you're being utterly ridiculous."

"No, she isn't," said Dave.

"What?" Carrie could hardly believe it. Even her best friend was siding with the smug ginger-haired giant.

"Carrie," Dave said, "think about it. You're the one who uncovered the trick the placktoids were pulling against the oootoon. You're the one who discovered that they were coercing the squashpumps into demanding reparations from the dandrobians. It was you who freed the hostages on the water planet, where they were defeated yet again. You've always been the one who stood in their way. It isn't Earth the placktoids are interested in, it's you."

"Well," said Belinda, "our planet does happen to be positioned somewhat strategically, but I would agree. Carrie was certainly a frequent topic of conversation among the dandrobians."

I'm right here, Carrie thought.

"Though I didn't hear it said in so many words," Belinda went on, "you're right, Dave. She has always been the fly in the ointment. I believe the placktoids intend to take Carrie out of the equation entirely."

Carrie swallowed. The meeting was turning into an emotional roller coaster. She'd gone from annoyed to guilty to extremely uneasy in a matter of moments. "Oh, come on. If that was the case why didn't they kidnap me instead of the PM? Why didn't they turn up at my factory? That would have been the perfect opportunity."

"Maybe that would have been too easy," Dave said. "You know the placktoids. They're over-confident and evil. They probably think they can capture you whenever they want. They haven't tried yet because they want you to suffer."

"If you were trying to make me feel better," said Carrie, "that probably wasn't the best thing to say."

"Sorry," Dave said. There was an uncomfortable pause. "Shall I make some more tea?"

CHAPTER NINETEEN

"I really don't think you should be doing this," said Dave.

The soldier fastened Carrie's safety harness and double-checked it.

"One of us has to help investigate these tunnels," Carrie replied. "Belinda's busy being debriefed by Errruorerrrrrh and you've got enough on your plate supervising the Unity troops and liaising with the police and the armed forces. Besides, the Unity starships will be here soon. We won't have time to think once they arrive. There's going to be no denying the existence of aliens when Earth's astronomers notice freaking great starships bearing down on us."

Dave grimaced. "I can't deny it. To give credit where it's due, the authorities have done a great job keeping panic levels at a minimum while the rampaging robots crisis—" he mimed quotation marks with his fingers "—goes on. All hell's going to break loose once people realise that evil extraterrestrial life forms really are out to get them."

"So the sooner we get to the bottom of this the better." Carrie looked down into the hole in the factory floor that she was about to descend. She added, "And I don't only mean that figuratively."

"Ready when you are, ma'am," the soldier said. "Have you ever abseiled before?"

"Yes," Carrie replied. "At least I think I have. This is how you do it, right?" She checked her line was secure then jumped into the hole. She bounced down the wall, paying out the rope, until she hit the bottom of the hole about ten metres below. Above her, Dave and the soldier were silhouetted against the factory lights.

"Er, yes ma'am," came the soldier's voice, echoing down. "That's how you do it."

Carrie unfastened her safety harness and stepped out of it. Sweeping her headlamp around, she saw four dark, round exits and the army squad and two Unity soldiers who were going to join her in the expedition.

"Carrie," Dave called.

"What?"

"Be careful."

"Of course. See you later."

She shouldered the placktoid-penetrating weapon she had borrowed from the Unity team and said to the squad sergeant, "Let's go."

Carrie, the soldiers and the two Unity troops set off down the tunnel. The Unity troops went first, followed by Carrie, the sergeant, then the six army privates who made up the squad.

Deep down, Carrie knew the task she had set herself wasn't particularly useful. People who understood much more about tunnels than she did had already carried out preliminary surveys and would soon return with more equipment and manpower to undertake a detailed, thorough search.

But her mood was very low and she needed to do something, anything, to take her mind off the fact that it was almost certainly her fault that Earth was being invaded. And not only that—she had also failed to do anything to stop it. In fact, she might have made the situation worse. Matthias Cowper had been interviewed by the police and they'd released him without charge, probably because he'd been thoroughly forewarned by her visit.

Still, perhaps she might find something significant in the tunnel. She couldn't make things worse, that was for sure.

"Did you help with the first search of the tunnels?" Carrie asked the army sergeant.

"I did," he replied. "I expect we won't find anything different this time around, I'm sorry to say, ma'am."

"Just a straight path for kilometres?"

"Yes, ma'am."

"Call me Carrie, please."

As they went along, she was reminded of her time inside the living mountain on the placktoids' planet, where the mechanical aliens' ancestors had toiled, maintaining the functions of their creators. If their heritage was anything to go by, the current-day plactoids would be very at home underground.

The tunnel was round and its walls were smooth, as if it had been bored by a single machine created specifically for the purpose. The preliminary report had stated that the tunnels had been constructed at a depth that avoided all sewer and utility pipes and cables as well as most building foundations. The report had also said that at that depth, vibrations from the construction would have been minimal at the surface, despite the heavy machinery required.

The finding in the report that bothered Carrie the most, however, was that the tunnels appeared to have been created heading into and not out from her factory. The third-generation plactoids and their babies hadn't escaped, they'd been rescued. While on the one hand that vindicated Carrie's hunch that the plactoids did care about their offspring and they would have been an effective bargaining tool if she and the authorities had acted sooner, it also meant that the plactoids were constructing an entire network of tunnels beneath UK soil. Four of them had converged at the factory. They had to have come from different directions.

It explained why the police and armed services hadn't been able to find the plactoids. The aliens had literally gone to ground. It also meant that the entire country was vulnerable to a sudden attack. Plactoids could spring from the ground at any moment, anywhere. Carrie shuddered.

The Unity troops leading the party halted and lifted their weapons to their shoulders. The sergeant raised his hand and, as one, Carrie and the squaddies also stopped. She couldn't see anything up ahead, despite the beams of many powerful head torches penetrating the darkness. But the Unity soldiers hadn't been alerted by something they'd seen. They'd felt something, and Carrie felt it too. The ground was vibrating.

The sergeant ordered his men to ready their weapons. They dropped to kneeling positions. Carrie also lifted her weapon to her shoulder. They had come far enough down the tunnel to be out of range of radio contact with the surface. Carrie had seniority. It was up to her to decide whether to investigate further or retreat. She told the Unity troops to advance slowly.

She followed them.

"Ma'am..." said the sergeant.

"Give us five minutes," she told him. "If we don't come back, return to the factory and request Unity reinforcements." The soldiers' weapons were useless against placktoids. She didn't want to send them into danger, and she didn't want the placktoids to discover that human weapons wouldn't harm them.

"Yes, ma'am," replied the sergeant, though Carrie could still hear a protesting tone in his voice. The boots of the retreating British soldiers echoed in the tunnel. The underground vibration was growing stronger.

Carrie's helmet contained a translation device that allowed her to communicate with the two Unity soldiers.

"Were you two among the troops who rescued me from the warehouse?" she asked.

"Yes," came the replies in unison.

"The devices you fought then were small and easy to defeat. The ones that have invaded this planet are much larger and tougher. I want you to understand that."

"Yes, we understand."

Now that the soldiers had left, the light of the combined beams of the three remaining headlamps was much dimmer. Beyond five or six metres ahead, the darkness was complete. The vibrations were growing stronger, and Carrie realised that she could also hear a deep bass hum. The noise was increasing. Something large and mechanical was approaching them.

In the smooth-walled tunnel, there was nowhere to hide. What was more, their headlamps would give them away instantly. Carrie silently cursed her own stupidity. "Activate infrared vision," she told the Unity soldiers and turned on her own.

Instantly the world turned deep, purplish-red and the Unity soldiers were transformed into glowing figures. Strangely, though the infrared vision extended much farther than the visible light of their headlamps, Carrie still couldn't see anything approaching.

The placktoids might not be technically alive, Carrie reasoned, but they had to emit some kind of light.

Her heart beat faster. It was like they were walking towards the enemy blindfolded. It was insanely dangerous. But if they retreated, they might miss out on the opportunity to discover something important. She signalled to the two Unity soldiers to stop. They drew to a halt. "Whatever it is that's heading our way hasn't seen us yet," she said softly into her mic, "or it would have sped up or fired on us. We'll wait here while it approaches. Meanwhile, prepare to retreat on my order."

They waited at the side of the tunnel while the vibrations grew stronger and the hum louder. Within less than a minute, the ground felt like it was jumping beneath Carrie's feet and her ears ached from the hum, yet still there was no sign of the approaching machine. Had the placktoids invented a cloaking device?

Carrie was about to give the order to retreat when she heard tapping on the top of her helmet. Dust and debris began to rain down from above. She looked up. Her infrared vision showed a glowing spinning point emerging from the tunnel wall.

"Run," she shouted as she realised what was happening. She sped away, retreating the way they had come. One of the soldiers came with her, but the other ran in the opposite direction. As soon as she noticed, she called out, "No! This way."

A tunneling machine was coming through the wall, headed by a massive drill. It was fast and it was insanely loud. Whether the soldier heard Carrie's command or whether he realised his error on his own, he came hurtling through the remaining gap just in time.

A second later, the machine broke through the wall, filling the entire tunnel. Carrie and the Unity soldiers ran.

CHAPTER TWENTY

The atmosphere at the meeting was grim. In other circumstances, Carrie would have been excited and awed to be present at a gathering that included the heads of the British military forces, the Deputy Prime Minister, the German Chancellor, the President of France and other European and African political leaders. Even the President of the United States was present via video phone—placktoids had been sighted in Manhattan. Listening in on the meeting were leaders of nations as yet unaffected by the placktoids.

Errruorerrrrrhch was also listening in and contributing, though only via audio link. It had been decided that her presence would be too alarming and a distraction for the dignitaries who had never seen a Transgalactic Council manager.

Earth was about to fall to the placktoids, and no one knew what to do about it. The tunnels that might have been the key to finding the secret location of the mechanical aliens had turned into a dead end. They ran in such a gigantic labyrinth under the UK that tunnel experts estimated it would take weeks to search them. Also, conducting the search was highly dangerous. The plactoids could have planted mines and triggers to set off bombs, which would also endanger whoever was living or working on the surface.

Yet everyone had agreed that the search that had already begun should continue with all possible speed. It was the only option they had. The problem was, they didn't have weeks to search for the plactoids. They had to locate the British Prime Minister with the utmost urgency, assuming she was still alive. It was also critical that the flow of plactoids across the globe was stemmed. They had to be prevented from making their next leap to a full-scale galactic invasion.

No one offered up a suggestion on how to do any of those things.

The assembled leaders of Earth seemed to have given up, repeating that they pinned their hopes on the Unity. Their starships were only hours away. When they arrived, they could use their superior technology to destroy the plactoids wherever they found them.

Carrie dreaded the idea of hordes of extraterrestrial soldiers roaming Earth and engaging in firefights with mechanical aliens. It would terrify entire populations. Millions would flee their homes, creating refugee crises on an unprecedented scale. Work and trade would cease. Economies would collapse. The panic that would ensue as the battle for the planet took place risked setting human societies back hundreds of years.

The prospect depressed her profoundly. And as if that wasn't enough to deal with, her cold was worse than ever. She thought she might even have the 'flu. Her eyes wouldn't stop watering, her nose was dripping like a tap and she had crusty sores under both nostrils. The corners of her lips were cracked from breathing through her mouth all the time, and her head felt like it was about to burst.

The meeting was drawing to a close and the British Deputy Prime Minister was summing up. The heads of state who didn't speak English listened to translations through their earpieces. Carrie pitied the leaders of the smaller countries. Many of them hadn't known about the Transgalactic Council or the existence of alien life. They'd barely had time to get used to those facts before they received the news that the Earth was being invaded and galactic war was about to break out.

Dave caught Carrie's eye from the other side of the room. She gave him a faint smile. It was all she could muster. She didn't think she could feel any worse. She had failed at defeating the placktoids, who were probably there because of her, and she had the most awful cold in the history of humankind.

The final words went to Errruorerrrrrhch. "Leaders of Earth, we at the Transgalactic Council understand that this is a challenging crisis for your citizens. It is perhaps the most challenging crisis they have ever faced. We pledge our full support to help you fight this threat, through the military might of the Unity. We are determined to eradicate the placktoids from your planet and return your civilisation to peace and prosperity. Together, we can beat the placktoids. Together, we can win."

Errruorerrrrrhch's words were rousing, but they seemed to have little effect on the mood of those present. Deep concern was etched on the faces of the men and women as the meeting broke up and the dignitaries were escorted out.

Dave was making his way around the large room towards her. Carrie dabbed gingerly at her nose with a tissue as she waited for him.

"Are you ready to go back to the flat?" he asked when he reached her. "Phwoah!" He grabbed his nose. "What's that smell?"

"What smell? I can't smell anything."

"It smells like garlic. Really bad."

"Oh, sorry. That's me. I've been chewing raw cloves. It's the only thing that helps with this cold, but even garlic doesn't do much. Can we stop at a pharmacy on the way back? I need to get some more tissues. And Vicks. And Lemsip."

"Okay. But I'm leaving the car window open."

They went out of the meeting room and eased through the crush of people who had stopped to discuss the momentous emergency.

Dave said, "Looks like we're out of the picture for a while. Now that the pressure's off, maybe you'll get better."

"Do you think we won't have anything to do now

that war's about to start?" Carrie asked. "We're still Transgalactic Council representatives. We'll have to continue in that role. We don't have a choice. If Council managers have to come here there really will be mass panic."

"Yeah, I'm not saying we can take a break, but I don't think we'll have much to do," Dave said. "Besides, Belinda will get stuck in and shoulder a lot of the work. You know what she's like."

"I do." Usually, Carrie would have hated the idea of the half-dandrobian taking over, but she was so tired, ill and despondent she really didn't care *what* Belinda did.

They took the lift down to the basement car park. When they arrived at Carrie's car, Dave offered to drive. She didn't object. He left the window closed. It was much too cold outside to open it. They went through the security gate and pulled into the London traffic, which was crawling. It was rush hour and already dark. Snow had begun to fall, promising to slow the traffic further. Warm air gushed from the dashboard vents, and the engine vibrations and steady swiping of the windscreen wipers soon sent Carrie into a doze.

When she woke, they were still driving. She sat up and checked the time. Over an hour had passed yet they were only just turning into their road.

Dave glanced at her. "How are you feeling? I stopped and got those things you wanted."

"Thanks. It's taken us ages to get here. Was the traffic really bad?"

"It was a nightmare, but never mind. We're here

now. I'll make us some dinner. Then if I were you I'd head straight to bed."

"Sounds like a good idea. I'm still tired even though I just slept."

"You're probably more sick than tired. You need to concentrate on getting better. Earth has some hard times coming up."

Carrie looked out of the window and up into the black sky. Snow was swirling down and the stars and moon were hidden behind thick clouds. "I wonder how far out the Unity starships are?"

"They'll be here by early morning at the latest," said Dave. "When we wake up tomorrow, the world will be a different place. Everything will have changed forever."

"Dave, do you think the Unity can defeat the placktoids?"

He drove into a parking spot and turned off the engine. He was silent for a while. "Honestly, Carrie, I don't know. Every time we think we've crushed those robots, they turn up again somewhere else. They always find a way out or another place to hide. They always rebuild their resources and attack again. Sometimes, it feels like they're unstoppable. Maybe it's because they're mechanical. Maybe it's actually impossible for us living beings to defeat them."

"Do you really think that could be true?" Carrie's last thread of hope was slipping away. Dave always seemed to be right about everything. What if he was right about this?

"What I'm trying to say is," Dave replied, "the

plactoids could be the next evolutionary step. Organic life forms could have reached the end of their domination of the galaxy."

"The dandrobians might have something to say about that."

"Granted," Dave said. "But they're play boys and girls. As long as they can hop from planet to planet, enjoying themselves, I don't think they'll care about much else. Their desire to escape was all about wanting freedom from monotony. Their lust for galactic domination seems to have faded away. I doubt they'll present much opposition to the plactoids."

"I hope you're wrong," said Carrie. "I'd hate to live in a galaxy run by megalomaniac mechanical aliens."

"Me too." Dave took the keys from the ignition and handed Carrie the bag of items he'd bought for her. "They'll probably insist on autonomy for all electronic appliances, and my washing machine talking back at me would get old really quick." He opened his door and an icy blast of snow-filled wind gusted in.

They went inside the block of flats. The lift was broken, so they climbed the stairs to the fourth floor. Carrie was looking forward to getting back to their flat. She had only one final night of peace before, as Dave had put it, everything would change forever. She wanted to enjoy the last few hours of normality with her pets.

When they reached the flat, they froze. The door had been busted wide open. It swung at a crazy angle from its lower hinge. Snow had blown into the hall and settled in a small drift.

Carrie's heart stopped. Her bag of pharmacy goods hit the floor. A glass bottle inside it shattered. She ran into the flat.

"Rogue," she yelled. "Rogue! Toodles!" She ran from room to room. Carrie called her pets' names over and over. She searched everywhere, lifting the beds and looking under them, opening the wardrobes, searching the cupboards. She couldn't find Rogue or Toodles. Aside from the overturned and broken furniture, all was dark and quiet. No answering bark or miaow came.

They were gone.

"Carrie," Dave called from the living room. He'd turned on the light, and he was standing next to the overturned coffee table. He held out a piece of paper that Carrie hadn't noticed during her search. She couldn't understand what he was doing. How could a piece of paper be important when her precious pets had run away and were lost? Then she noticed his face. It was drained of colour.

Carrie took the paper. A message was printed on it. CARRIE HATCHETT, WE HAVE YOUR ANIMALS. GIVE YOURSELF UP OR THEY WILL DIE.

CHAPTER TWENTY-ONE

As Dave handed Carrie the message from the placktoids, he dreaded her response. If he'd learned anything about her in the time they'd been friends, it was that she loved her pets very much, probably more than life itself.

Carrie was already a mess. Her apparently incurable cold had made her look terrible, and her hair was even more tangled and unkempt than usual. But the simple common cold and a bad hair day was nothing compared to the potential effect of the news that her pets had been kidnapped.

She was staring blankly at the paper, frozen in position. A single watery drop of mucus clung to the end of her nose.

"Carrie?"

She didn't move. She didn't speak. Dave wasn't sure if she had forgotten to breathe.

"Carrie."

Not a twitch.

"Maybe you should sit down."

Finally, she moved. She bent to put the paper down on the coffee table. Only the table was overturned, the ends of its legs poking up in the air. Still, she let go of the paper as if she was placing it carefully on the original surface. The paper fluttered to the floor.

She turned to leave.

"Where are you going?"

She didn't seem to hear him at first. Then, as if in afterthought, she turned back. "Where's your toolkit?" she asked. "Do you remember?" Her voice was calm, as if she were only asking out of interest.

"I put it in my wardrobe," Dave replied, "but I don't know if it's still there. Why?"

Without answering, Carrie left the room. Dave hurried after her, wondering what her plan was—*worrying* what her plan was.

She went into his bedroom and straight over to the wardrobe. His Liaison Officer toolkit was where he'd left it, on a high shelf. The placktoids might have recognised the bag—they'd taken it from him during his previous Council assignment—but if they had, they hadn't been interested in it. They had probably only wanted Carrie's pets.

The realisation struck him like an ice-pick to the heart. Not only had they somehow figured out how to hurt Carrie the most, they also wanted her dead. They'd known she would come after her pets at all costs, recklessly risking herself to get them back. They hadn't even bothered telling her where to go. They knew she would find them.

She lifted down the bag and, without asking if she could borrow it, put it over her shoulder. She went past him into the hall and out the open front door.

"Carrie," Dave called as he rushed to catch up to her. If he didn't make her calm down and think about her actions, she would do something rash and illogical. She had a reputation for it. "Carrie, where are you going? I've got the car keys, remember?"

Something of his meaning must have penetrated because, after a few more steps, she stopped and about-faced. Her expression was stony as she held out her hand. When he didn't immediately hand over the keys, she said, "Give them to me."

"Wait. Just a minute," he said. "We need to think this through. We need a plan."

Carrie calmly walked up to him. "Give them to me," she repeated tonelessly, "or I'll take them from you."

Though Carrie was a head shorter than him and a woman, Dave knew only too well that she could easily beat him in a fight. He fished in his pocket for the keys. "If you would just c—" The words 'calm down' died on his lips as he caught the look in his friend's eyes. There was something in there that he'd never seen before. Something that frightened him.

He handed her the keys. Without a word, she took them and continued to stride to the stairs. Dave guessed the placktoids might have had something to do with the lift not working. He glanced at the door to the flat. It was swinging in the chill winter wind. He should go back and close it. He should fix it so that the flat was secure. If he didn't, it wouldn't take long for the local lowlifes to walk right in and loot the place. He should go back and remove his valuables at the very least.

He ran after Carrie.

She was speeding down the stairs. With some difficulty, he caught up as she reached the bottom. "I don't know where you're going," he panted, "but I'm coming with you."

He might as well have not existed for all the acknowledgement he received of his words. Carrie unlocked the car and got into the driving seat. Dave ran around to the other side and opened the passenger door. He only just had time to climb in before Carrie had started the engine and pulled away. He reached to grab the passenger door as it swung out. As Carrie took a corner, he pulled it closed. She left the car park at high speed and apparently without looking for oncoming traffic.

"Carrie," Dave exclaimed. "Watch what you're doing. You're going to get us both killed."

She didn't reply, but his words seemed to register. Her speed slowed a fraction, and she looked from side to side as well as straight ahead. The evening traffic was still terrible. Carrie went down side streets and narrow one-way alleys as she circumvented the traffic jams, apparently intuitively. Whenever they hit an open stretch of road, she floored the accelerator heedless of flashing speed cameras. She raced through traffic lights as they changed.

Dave recognised the streets they were travelling. They were heading back the way they had come, returning to Scotland Yard. But he had a feeling that Carrie wasn't going there to alert the Commissioner to the placktoids' note. She wouldn't be asking him to mount a coordinated search and rescue mission for her pets. That would have been the reaction of someone in their right mind.

No. What had been professional had become personal. Carrie was going to solve this problem, and she was going to do it her way and on her own terms. Which, Dave knew from experience, meant they were in uncharted territory.

She pulled up on a double red line outside Scotland Yard.

"You can't stop here," Dave exclaimed. "They'll tow us in minutes. Then they'll probably arrest us."

But Carrie was already getting out of the car. She crossed the pavement and went inside the headquarters of the Metropolitan Police. Dave cursed to himself and craned his neck around to watch the traffic that was building up behind Carrie's car. Drivers tooted loud and long as they struggled to pass on the busy road.

It was no good. He would have to move the car. He would park it in the basement and return on foot to tell Carrie where it was.

Dave climbed over the gear stick and into the

driver's seat. Reaching forward and feeling at the side of the steering column, he cursed again. Carrie had taken the keys with her. Resigned, he returned to the passenger side and fastened his seat belt. A driver wound down his window and uttered an expletive-filled rant as he sped past. Dave slid low in his seat.

Then Carrie was back, and she was armed. She kicked the rear passenger door. Dave got the hint and reached over the seats to open it. Carrie threw in the weapons and shut the door before returning to the driver's seat. Somehow, she'd managed to procure several Unity-made, placktoid-penetrating weapons. Dave didn't know how she'd got them past security at Scotland Yard, but he did know there was no point in asking.

Carrie started the car. Dave almost didn't recognise his best friend. Her lips were a thin line and her eyes were set and focused. All kindness and softness had disappeared from her features. Her nose had even stopped running.

Dave gripped the door handle as they swerved through the streets of London. The traffic finally began to clear. The snow had stopped, and the black clouds were departing. Faint stars competed with the bright street lamps as the night turned frosty.

He looked about, trying to figure out where they were going. A few streets later, he guessed. They were heading for Broadcasting House. Carrie was returning to the headquarters of the BBC. It was a good idea. She was going to find the dandrobians and get the information she needed from them. If anyone knew where the placktoids were it was the dandrobians. They might even know where the mechanical aliens had taken Rogue and Toodles. Despite her apparent ice-cold fury, Carrie was thinking straight.

The car whizzed around yet another corner, sending Dave into the door. He was beginning to feel sick. Carrie pushed herself backward in her seat and locked her left leg as she slammed on the brakes. Dave braced himself against the dashboard. A screech and the smell of burning rubber came from beneath the car. They'd stopped in front of Broadcasting House.

Carrie reached into the back seat and grabbed a weapon. She handed it to Dave. He took it. Even in her current state, she knew he would stick with her. She got out and retrieved the rest of the weapons, slinging them over her shoulders. The larger guns dwarfed her, but as she marched up to the entrance doors, she moved easily as if they weighed nothing.

Carrie lifted a weapon and sighted it. Without bothering to check whether the door was locked, she blew it apart. Stepping over the smoking remains, she went inside and pointed the muzzle at the receptionist. The man instantly disappeared beneath his desk.

Carrie fired on the door next to him and reduced it to a smouldering ruin. She was inside the BBC. Dave followed.

CHAPTER TWENTY-TWO

A fog of mental images of her pets was drifting through Carrie's mind. Rogue was bounding up to her, his tail wagging. Toodles was winding around her legs or nuzzling into her lap. The images played over and over. Carrie shook her head.

She had to concentrate on her mission to rescue her dog and cat, and kill anyone who tried to stop her.

Before he ducked behind his desk, Carrie had recognised the receptionist as the same one who had been present when she'd met Matthias Cowper. She briefly considered returning to the lobby, hauling the man to his feet and demanding that he tell her where to find the dandrobian and his accomplices. But she didn't need him She could find them herself.

"Matthias Cowper," she shouted. A head appeared out of a doorway. The person's eyes popped at the sight of Carrie bearing her many weapons. The head withdrew and the door slammed shut.

As Carrie strode the corridors of the BBC, she became vaguely aware of metallic clicks. They were sounding out ahead of her as she went along. *Metallic clicks? It had to be placktoids.* She lifted her weapon, ready to aim. Then she recognised the sound. It wasn't placktoids. It was the locks on the doors being closed as she approached.

Cowper had to be there somewhere. He wouldn't have gone home yet. He would have stayed at work, where he and the other dandrobians could hatch their plans. They would help the placktoids when the Unity troops deployed. They had to know the Unity was coming. The dandrobians knew everything.

"Matthias Cowper," Carrie yelled.

Dave was somewhere behind her. He would back her up. He would help her find Rogue and Toodles. Her vision was clouding again with her beloved, innocent friends. Carrie had always known the placktoids were evil, but she had never imagined they would stoop this low. If they could hurt harmless animals, who knew what else they might do? They had to be stopped.

"Matthias Cowper," Carrie roared. "Get out here you son of a b—"

A door opened. The dandrobian stepped out, smiling. Positively grinning, in fact. Carrie fought the urge to blow his head off. He could tell her where Rogue and Toodles were. He was going to tell her everything.

She stalked towards him, aiming the muzzle of her

weapon between his eyes. His smile fell and he broke into an instant sweat. Lifting his hands, he said, "Now then, darling, no need to—"

Carrie placed the muzzle point on his forehead. "Where are my friends?"

"Your friends?" Cowper echoed. He seemed genuinely puzzled. "I'm afraid I don't understand."

"Where are my animals? My pets?"

"You think of your animals as—"

"Where are they?" Carrie barked. She pushed her gun into the dandrobian's head, forcing him backward and against the door frame.

A muted cry and a scuffling sound came from behind her. Cowper looked beyond Carrie, and the corner of his lips lifted in a smirk. What was he looking at? Was it a bluff? Carrie chanced a glance over her shoulder. Dandrobians had put a bag over Dave's head and were struggling with him on the floor. They had sneaked up while she was threatening Cowper.

Carrie spun to face him again, but it was too late. Cowper was fast, and he was much larger and stronger than her. He wrested her weapon from her hands and threw a bag over her head. Darkness descended. With a grip like iron he forced her wrists together behind her back and pushed her to her knees.

Unbearable pressure was put on her shoulders. She collapsed onto the carpet. Carrie fought and raged, but there was nothing she could do. Her wrists were tied. More hands joined Cowper's and soon she was trussed like a chicken about to be roasted. The dandrobians picked her up and carried her away. Carrie stopped struggling. It was pointless, and she was only wasting energy. Brute force and weaponry had failed her, but she still had her brains.

"Now there's a sensible girl," said Cowper. "If you struggle, you'll only hurt yourself. And we don't want to hurt you, dear." He added, "We'll leave that to the placktoids." He and the others laughed.

Blinded by the bag over her head, she counted Cowper's steps and the number and directions of the turns they took. Something squeaked—a door was opening. She was carried down some steps. The air was cooler and moister. They seemed to be going into a seldom-used basement.

Another door opened and hit the wall behind it with a bang. She was thrown onto a cold concrete floor. Before Carrie could even rise to her knees, the door closed. A key turned in the lock.

She inched across the floor until she hit a wall. By rubbing her head repeatedly against it, she finally managed to work the bag off her head. It didn't make much difference to her predicament—the room was entirely dark.

"Hello?" Carrie held a faint hope that Dave might have been put in the same room. No answer came. Shuffling on her bottom, she crossed the floor from wall to wall until she figured out the room was around three metres square and empty.

The Carrie of that afternoon—sick, depressed about her failure to defeat the placktoids and worried about the upcoming war— that Carrie might have despaired at her situation. But this was not that Carrie. This one was different. This was a Carrie whose pets had been taken from her. Somewhere deep within her subconscious, a line had been crossed.

She wasn't about to waste time cursing her fate or fearing what might happen. Failure was not a word in her dictionary. She would escape. She would save her pets. It was only a matter of when and how. She would rescue Toodles and Rogue or die trying.

Yet determination wouldn't open a locked door or break through walls. She would have to think of another way out. The dandrobians could never be persuaded to let her go, that was certain. They had no incentive to help her and they had plenty to gain from their alliance with the placktoids. Appealing to their better natures was also pointless—they had none. They were amoral, capricious, hedonistic and—what was it Belinda had said? Vain. Vain and arrogant. Two highly appropriate adjectives for the immortal aliens who had once ruled the galaxy.

Though they were brilliant and charismatic, the dandrobians had their weaknesses too. Perhaps Carrie could find a way to use them in her favour.

As she mulled over how to use her knowledge of the dandrobians to help her escape, she recalled another arrow in her quiver: Dave. He'd been captured too. With the two of them working together, they could surely escape and find her pets. But where was he?

Carrie shuffled across the room to the door.

"Dave," she shouted. "Can you hear me?"

His answer was immediate. "Carrie! I was worried about what happened to you."

"Now then," a voice called out. "You two are not to talk to each other." Footsteps came down the corridor and Carrie's door was unlocked. She screwed up her eyes in the sudden light. A male dandrobian stood in the doorway, his hands on his hips. "Well, well, well. Aren't you the clever one? How did you remove your bag? I'm afraid that isn't—*ooof.*"

Carrie had been kneeling just inside the door. She'd thrown herself at the alien's legs, knocking him down. She executed a forward roll so she could kick the downed dandrobian's head with the heels of her tied feet. But her prison keeper wasn't alone. Matthias Cowper came speeding to his partner's aid. Before Carrie could strike her blow, he lifted her and threw her back into the room.

She hit the floor head first. The impact dazed her. Cowper was next to her in two strides. He roughly put the bag over her head once more.

"What a vicious little vixen you are," he said. "It's no wonder the placktoids want to put a permanent end to your constant interference." He tightened the ties on the bag until it was uncomfortably tight around her neck. "Personally, I find the execution of enemies distasteful and rather unsporting, but in your case I'm prepared to make an exception."

Carrie heard him stand and return to the door. "Narcissus, darling, are you all right? I do hope you aren't hurt."

Narcissus?

Carrie could hardly believe her luck. But she had to act quickly.

"Narcissus?" she asked. "Not *the* Narcissus, surely?"

"Yes, I am," came the dandrobian's reply, sounding aggrieved.

"I'm so sorry," Carrie said. "If I'd known who you were, I would never have touched you. Please accept my apology."

She could hear the figure from Ancient Greek mythology getting to his feet. "It would be churlish of me, in the circumstances, not to forgive you," he replied. "Your apology is accepted."

"Thank you. And, would it be too much to ask if I might take a look at you, Narcissus? Just a quick one. You're extremely famous in Earth history, you see."

"I really don't think that's such a good idea," Cowper interjected.

"Oh, go on," said Narcissus. "Be a dear and let her. It's entirely understandable that she would want to look at me. It won't hurt."

Cowper sighed a world-weary sigh, as if he was well-used to Narcissus', well, narcissism.

"And, if he's Narcissus," Carrie went on, "might I ask your true name, Matthias?"

The dandrobian sighed as if bored by her question, though not convincingly so. "If you must know, I'm Adonis."

Jackpot.

CARRIE'S CALAMITY

CHAPTER TWENTY-THREE

"No, I really can't," said Carrie. "It's impossible. You're both as good-looking as each other."

Carrie hadn't only managed to persuade Cowper/Adonis to remove the bag on her head, she'd also bent the conversation to which of the two gorgeous dandrobians was the most handsome. She had the distinct feeling that the question was one that each of the aliens had thoroughly explored, if not aloud, then definitely within their immortal minds.

An eternity of comparing yourself to someone else, Carrie thought. Immortality didn't seem so attractive.

"Oh you're just being polite," Narcissus said to her. "One of us must have the edge. You can tell us. We don't really mind, do we, Adonis?"

"No, not at all," Adonis replied through his teeth.

"I've got an idea," Carrie said brightly. "Why don't we ask my friend Dave? You dandrobians all look amazingly attractive to us, but Dave's a bit of a connoisseur of good-looking men. So I've heard."

"You mean that human who came here with you?" asked Narcissus. "That *is* a good idea. He's rather dishy himself. I felt quite guiilty capturing him like that. Though his looks aren't quite in my or Adonis' league, are they darling?"

Adonis gave a dismissive shake of his head, as if Narcissus was mad to even suggest such a thing.

"I'll get him," said Narcissus cheerfully. He went to the door diagonally opposite, drawing a bunch of keys from his pocket.

"I don't suppose you could untie my ankles?" Carrie asked Adonis when Narcissus went into the room where Dave was imprisoned. "They're getting very sore."

"Of course I couldn't," replied the dandrobian. "It's out of the question."

"Oh, please. It isn't like I could escape, is it? I could never get away from you. You're much bigger, stronger and faster than me. You must be the fittest dandrobian I've ever seen."

"Well..." Adonis, who had worn a frown ever since Carrie had failed to choose him as the most handsome compared to Narcissus, began to look pleased.

"I was hoping you might agree if I asked nicely," Carrie said. "I've heard so many stories about your benevolence and mercy."

"Really?" The corner of the alien's mouth lifted in a half-smile. "There are stories about me, are there? Tell me, are there many?"

"Hundreds," Carrie replied. Then, when Adonis' smile began to fall, she corrected herself. "Thousands, I mean. Most of our stories set in ancient times are about you, in fact."

"How remarkable. And what do the stories say?" Adonis bent down to unbind Carrie's ankles.

Carrie was about to make up some flattering nonsense—the truth was, she couldn't remember much on the myths about Adonis except that he was an extremely beautiful youth—when Narcissus returned with Dave.

"Did you hear that?" Adonis asked Narcissus. "Most of their stories of the time we were here are about me."

"Oh," Narcissus looked disappointed. "Is that so?" he asked Carrie.

"Errm...to be honest, I didn't do very well in history at school. Why don't we ask Dave? And he can settle the question as to which of you two is the most handsome at the same time."

Dave, who was standing precariously with his feet tied together, jerked his head in response to this proposal. His head was covered in a bag, but his discomfiture was clear.

"Yes," exclaimed Narcissus. "Let's."

He undid the tie on the bag and pulled it off. Dave's normally well-groomed hair was ruffled and sticking up with static. He blinked as his eyes got used to the light. "Sorry, I was crap at history too, but you want me to judge which of our kidnappers is the most handsome?"

"Yes," Carrie replied, as if it was the most ordinary

question in the world. "But first, let me introduce you. Dave, meet Narcissus, and this is Adonis."

Dave replied with a drawn out *Ohhhh* as an inkling of what Carrie was trying to do dawned on him. "Right. Who's the most good-looking? Hmmm, let me see."

"Wait," Carrie said. "Wouldn't it be best to untie Dave's feet too? He needs to be able to walk around you both so that he can look at you from all sides."

"Oh no," said Narcissus. "We must keep you both tied up. The placktoids will be here any minute. They won't like it at all if you aren't restrained." He noticed Carrie's unbound ankles. "Adonis, what were you thinking?"

"Narcissus," Adonis replied in a patronising tone, "how could they possibly get away from us? *They're* human and *we're* dandrobian. Think about it."

Narcissus' beautiful features twisted as he considered the question. His gaze went from human-size Carrie and Dave to exceptionally tall, well-built Adonis and himself. He took a moment to answer. Carrie had a feeling that Narcissus was lower than average in the intelligence stakes among dandrobians.

"I suppose you're right," he said. He untied Dave's ankle restraints. "Now..." He put his hands on his hips, rested his weight on one leg and thrust his nose into the air. "...what do you think?"

"Errr," Dave said. "Give me a minute. I need to get a proper look."

Adonis assumed a more casual pose. He leaned his back against the wall and folded his arms, as if he didn't care what Dave's decision might be. Carrie noticed, however, that he folded his fists under his biceps to make them more prominent. He gazed off to one side and opened his mouth slightly, looking like a catalogue model.

While Dave was pretending to assess the attractiveness of the two dandrobians, Carrie was sizing them up. Adonis' position put his head slightly lower than Narcissus'. She would go for him first. Despite the aliens' weaknesses of personality, they remained far her superiors physically. She wouldn't get more than one chance with either of them.

Dave's eyebrows were frantically questioning her. Carrie gave a slight nod towards Narcissus. Dave continued to look as though he had no idea what she needed him to do, but she couldn't risk any further communication. Hopefully he would get the idea when the time came.

Adonis was getting tired of holding his pose. He began to straighten up. "So, what do you—"

Carrie's kick hit him square on the side of his head. The move had been something of a stretch for her, but she'd made contact with her full force. He dropped without a sound.

"Wha...?" Narcissus looked around at the sound of the blow landing. His eyes went wide as he witnessed his fellow dandrobian fall to the floor.

"Hold him," Carrie shouted.

Dave grabbed Narcissus in a bear hug from behind. The dandrobian was far taller than Carrie. It would be a reach, but she had enough distance for a short run up. As Dave and Narcissus struggled, Carrie bounded over, leapt and kicked him in the head. This time, due to the forewarning Narcissus had, the blow didn't land as heavily as she'd wanted. It only slightly stunned the dandrobian.

When he staggered, Dave pushed him down. He fell against the wall. Now Carrie could reach him easily. With all the strength she could muster, she drove her heel into his face. Blood erupted from Narcissus' nose. He was out cold.

"Run," Carrie shouted. "This way."

CHAPTER TWENTY-FOUR

"Wait," Dave shouted. "I can hear something."

"We don't have time," Carrie called back as she ran. "Those two will come around any minute. We need to get out of here and rescue Toodles and Rogue before the placktoids do something terrible to them."

A few steps later, she checked that Dave was following. He wasn't. He was rummaging in the unconscious Narcissus' pockets. Carrie stopped.

"Dave," she yelled down the corridor. "What are you doing? Come on!"

But he didn't answer. He'd found what he was looking for. He went to one of the doors and, after trying a few keys, unlocked it.

"Thank goodness," said a woman's voice. She had a clipped accent. "I thought you might be one of those awful Beeb execs gone mental. But I heard the scuffling and thought it was safe to call out. Are you the police?"

"No," said Dave, "we were locked up too. We just escaped."

When the woman came out of the room, Carrie could hardly believe her eyes. She was a famous actor who played the lead role in a long-running, much-loved British science fiction series. Carrie had no time for fan-worship, however. The dandrobians were waking up.

"Dave," she called urgently.

"Sorry," he said to the actor, "we've got to go."

"I'll come with you," she replied. "I'm not sticking around here."

Carrie led Dave and the actor up the stairs and along the corridors, recalling the turns and numbers of steps she had memorized.

"What were you doing in there?" Dave asked the actor, panting as he ran. "Why were you locked up?"

"I might ask you two the same question," she replied. "My answer's simple enough, though perhaps you won't believe me. Those goons kidnapped and imprisoned me because I tried to expose them for what they are."

"Sorry?" Dave shared a look with Carrie.

"I informed the BBC higher-ups that we had aliens living and working amongst us."

"Aliens?" Dave asked.

"Believe me, I know how it must sound. I'd swear they thought my current role had gone to my head. They must have only been humoring me when they said they'd look into it. I doubt they really began an investigation, but word got out. The next thing I knew, I was being manhandled by those two extraterrestrials and their female accomplices and I was locked away. If you hadn't let me out, I don't know what would have happened to me."

Carrie asked, "You think Matthias Cowper is an alien?"

"No doubt you think I'm insane."

"No," Carrie replied. "Not at all." She was tempted to say more but bit her tongue. If the actor had seen through the dandrobians she was intelligent, and she seemed fit and strong from the way she ran. She also viewed the dandrobians as dangerous enemies, which meant she might be useful for what Carrie was certain lay ahead.

"I understand the difference between a television programme and reality as well as the next person," the actor continued, "perhaps better than most, given my job. But I'm positive there's something not-quite-human about those four. The fact that they wanted to silence me only confirms my suspicions."

"You've got a point," panted Dave.

They turned a corner. They had nearly returned to the spot where Carrie and Dave had been captured.

"Where are we going, by the way?" the woman asked. "Only, if you two aren't the police, I really ought to be phoning them right now."

"You can phone them soon," said Carrie. "It would be great if you would. But though we aren't the police, we're something similar. I think we're going to need your help."

"I see," the actor said. "I'm guessing we aren't quite out of our hole yet. Well, I'm all yours. I've only learned how to play fight, but I'll give it my all."

"Thanks," Carrie replied.

As they turned another corner, the sight that met them confirmed Carrie's prediction. The two female dandrobians were in the corridor waiting for them. She'd often suspected the dandrobians were telepathic. Narcissus and Adonis must have woken up and alerted their female counterparts. They'd arrived to cut off their escape.

Carrie, Dave and the actor skidded to a halt. The two female dandrobians looked formidable as they stood barring their way, taking up most of the corridor. Carrie pushed up her shirt sleeves. The actor did the same. Dave was bent over, clutching his knees as he caught his breath. Then he straightened up and faced the dandrobians with a mean look in his eye.

"There's no point in running," said one of the aliens. "The placktoids are almost here. Even if you get past us, you won't escape."

"If that's so," Carrie replied. "Why are you bothering to stop us leaving?"

The dandrobian's smug expression faltered and she gave her comrade a look that said, *why **are** we bothering to stop them*? Neither apparently had an answer for their response was to stride forward, arms outstretched.

In the few seconds remaining before the

dandrobians reached them, Carrie sized up the situation. If the dandrobians were telling the truth, they had very little time before the placktoids arrived in full force. Though finding them was Carrie's aim, she wanted it to be on her terms, not caught again like a rat in a trap. Tangling with the female dandrobians would only slow them down, and it would give Adonis and Narcissus time to catch up.

She whispered a hastily put-together plan to Dave and the actor.

As one, the three yelled at the tops of their voices before racing to meet the oncoming aliens head on. The ferocity of their advance surprised their enemies. The pair slowed and looked uncertain. They prepared to meet the humans by raising their arms in defence of the approaching attack.

At the final split second, Carrie and the others altered their trajectories and, rather than colliding with the dandrobians, they neatly side-stepped them and sped past. Only one of the aliens was quick enough to react in time to the trick. She grabbed the end of the actor's long coat, nearly pulling her off her feet. But the woman lifted her arms behind her so she slipped out of the coat, leaving it dangling in the dandrobian's hands.

The last Carrie saw of the aliens before they sped away was the dumbfounded expression of the one who had grabbed the coat.

They were nearly at the front of the building. If they could reach it before the dandrobians, they could use the car Carrie had left parked outside to escape, providing it hadn't been towed. She cursed the fact that the aliens had taken her weapons, but she would just have to do without them.

They reached the security door she had blown apart. The wreckage was faintly smoking. Stepping through the remains, they went into Broadcasting House's reception area. The receptionist was nowhere to be seen.

The remnants of the front doors that Carrie had destroyed were similarly undisturbed. They went through the open hole and out into the street. Carrie's eyes were focussed on the spot where she'd left the car. It was still there, she noted with relief. As she hurried towards it, however, Dave grabbed her upper arm, restraining her.

"Carrie," he said. His voice sounded oddly tight and nervous.

The actor had also halted. "Oh...my...goodness," she breathed.

Carrie peered into the darkness. It was only then that she realised it was unusually dark. All the street lights were out, and the road was entirely empty of traffic. As Carrie's eyes adjusted to the light, she finally saw what was disturbing her companions.

Ranged around them in a semi-circle were placktoids. Hundreds of them, big and small. Shredders were there, along with 3-D printers, paperclips, pens, and other unfamiliar types. A plackoid army had turned up to meet them.

CHAPTER TWENTY-FIVE

"Carrie Hatchett," screamed, squeaked, squealed and shrieked the surrounding placktoids in unison. The noise was almost unbearably painful. Carrie, Dave and the actor dropped to their knees, their hands over their ears.

"You are surrounded," the mechanical aliens continued, their voices echoing from the buildings around.

Keeping her hands over her ears, Carrie lifted her arm and checked behind her. On the steps of Broadcasting House, the four dandrobians stood. Their expressions were uncharacteristically grim. Narcissus' face was covered in dried blood. There would be no exit in that direction.

"You cannot escape us this time," the placktoids chorused. "We have you at last."

Rising to her feet, her hands forming fists as they fell

to her sides, Carrie shouted, "Where are my animals? If you've hurt a hair on either of them, I won't rest until I've hunted every last one of you down and destroyed you all."

"You will come with us," cried the placktoids. "You will menace us no more. When you are gone, our invasion will succeed without impediment. Come. Now."

"I'm not going anywhere until you tell me my pets are safe. Bring them here."

"No. You must come with us. We will not return your animals until then."

Carrie squeezed her eyes shut as she tried to block out the mental images of her beloved Toodles and Rogue at the mercy of those terrible machines.

"If I promise to go with you, will you release them?"

"What?" Dave exclaimed. "No! Carrie, you can't. They'll kill you."

Carrie's eyes filled with tears as she turned to her friend. "I have to do it, Dave. If Toodles or Rogue get hurt and I could have done something to stop it, I couldn't live with myself. The placktoids are right. We're trapped. They've got us right where they want us. If giving myself up is the only way to save my pets, that's what I have to do." She rubbed away a tear that had spilled onto her cheek. "And let my friends here go," she called to the placktoids. "You have to do that too."

"No," Dave shouted, also rising to his feet. "There's no way I'm leaving you."

"Me neither," said the actor. "I might have only just

met you two, but you saved me from a potentially slow, lingering death back in there. I'm sticking by you."

The placktoids seemed to engage in some silent electronic communication for a few moments. Then they spoke: "We will bring the animals here. Then you will go with us."

Carrie's reaction was a mixture of relief and puzzlement. She was joyful that Toodles and Rogue were alive and apparently unharmed, but she was also confused by how quickly the placktoids had agreed to her demands. They had the clear advantage. All they had to do was to fire one of their deadly weapons at them and it would all be over. Yet they had agreed to do as Carrie asked with little argument.

"And let the other humans go," she reminded them.

"I'm not going anywhere," said Dave forcefully. "You think I went through everything I did to just leave you like this? You think I suffered through all those times in Oootoon and Dandrobia and the water world for nothing? You think I went back in time to the placktoid planet with you and got ejected from a mountain to leave you? We nearly *died* together. Several times. Do you really think I put up with your reckless, irrational behaviour all this time just to abandon you now?" Despite Dave's harsh words, his lower lip was trembling and his expression was desperate and sad. "Don't do it, Carrie. We'll find a way out of this yet. You'll figure out a way. You always do."

Carrie hung her head. "I'm out of ideas this time, Bestie."

"There has to be a way," Dave said. He looked up at the sky. The placktoids' extinguishing of the street lights meant the glimmer of a few stars was visible in the darkness. Perhaps he was hoping that the Unity starships would arrive in the nick of time and save the day. But only the ancient constellations gleamed there. By the time the Unity arrived it would be too late for Carrie.

She'd promised herself she would rescue her pets or die trying. She wasn't going to break that promise.

A bark broke the silence. A very familiar bark. Carrie's heart soared. It was Rogue. He was okay. Her handsome dog came bounding through the placktoid ranks and leapt into Carrie's waiting arms. His kisses quickly wet her face and she struggled to hold onto him as he wriggled violently with excitement. Carrie dropped him gently down, then knelt and ruffled his neck, burying her face in it and breathing his slightly stinky doggie odor.

Something soft and warm pushed against her thigh. There was Toodles, purring and head-butting her as she demanded her share of attention. Carrie was in heaven. She stroked and petted her cat, scratching the top of her head just the way she liked it.

Carrie checked her animals over. Neither had a mark on them and they seemed none the worse for their ordeal. She pulled them both into her arms, tears flooding from her eyes at her relief that they were okay. They were safe and that was all that mattered. She could go now. They might miss her a little bit at first, but they would forget her eventually and be happy.

"You'll look after them, won't you?" she asked Dave.

"It isn't going to come to that," he replied through his teeth.

"They'll like your neighbour," Carrie said. "She's a lovely old lady. She'll give them treats. You like treats, don't you?" she asked Toodles and Rogue.

Rogue slurped her face in reply and Toodles miaowed, as if the mention of treats had given her an idea.

"We have fulfilled our side of the bargain," the placktoids chorused. "Now you must come with us."

"No," Dave shouted, "she isn't coming!"

"Don't tell them that," Carrie said to him as she stood up. "They could shoot any one of us down right this second if they wanted."

Dave grabbed his hair in frustration. "I can't believe this is happening. This isn't how things are supposed to turn out. No matter how bad things get, we always win in the end. Always."

"That's what happens in stories," said Carrie.

The placktoids in the center of the semi-circle were moving apart. A narrow pathway formed, bordered by the sharp edges and metallic limbs of the mechanical aliens. They were creating an exit for her. It was time to leave. But Carrie didn't trust the evil metal life forms.

"Let my friends go first," she called out. "I want to see them leave safely before I come with you."

A silent conference. "We agree."

"Carrie," Dave said, pleading.

"I think we should stay too," said the actor. "I'm not prepared to sneak away while you go off to an uncertain fate."

"Look," Carrie said angrily. "You two are the only chance I have of saving my pets. These aliens could kill us all at any moment. You have to leave now. Take Toodles and Rogue to safety for me. Please."

Dave's gaze held Carrie's until she thought her heart would break. "If you don't do this for me," she said to him. "I will never forgive you."

At her words, her best friend's resolve finally melted. He looked defeated. Dropping his gaze and holding out his hand he said, "Give me the keys."

Carrie took the car keys from her pocket and placed them in his palm. He pulled her into a tight hug. Then, without looking at her again, he grabbed Rogue's collar and began to tug him towards the car. Rogue resisted and pulled back, barking. Dave continued to drag him across the pavement, his claws scrabbling on the hard surface. The actor picked up Toodles. The cat miaowed plaintively.

Carrie watched her beloved pets and best friend as they got into the car. The actor sat in the back with Toodles. Dave seemed unable to look at Carrie as he drove away, the placktoids moving aside to let the car pass.

Swallowing her quickly rising fear, Carrie turned to the dark passage the placktoids had created for her. It was not the ending she'd hoped for. The mechanical aliens would not stop their invasion of the galaxy now that they finally had her in their clutches. On the contrary. Once she was out of the way, they would probably gain new confidence in rushing ahead with their plans.

What the future held in store for humanity, Carrie couldn't guess. She only hoped that Dave would be able to keep himself and her pets safe. In his position working for the Transgalactic Council, he might be able to swing a transfer to a safer world in a far-distant part of the galaxy. In view of her sacrifice, the Council would probably grant it.

As for Carrie, her fate was decided. She walked towards the waiting placktoids.

CHAPTER TWENTY-SIX

The mechanical aliens had taken over an old, disused warehouse in Canary Wharf. The place had somehow escaped the recent regeneration of the area. It stood at the end of a lane, recently fallen snow dusting its dark, ancient roof and the edges of broken window panes.

A placktoid in the shape of a giant paperclip had brought Carrie there, carrying her within its internal forcefield. She'd been transported to the placktoid spaceship in the same manner on her first assignment, so it seemed a fitting way to take her final journey with the evil aliens.

The paperclip had led the way across London to the warehouse, the others following in a kind of procession. The attention they had attracted stopped traffic, caused accidents and left pedestrians open-mouthed and frozen in shock. The fact that the placktoids were no longer bothering to hide spoke volumes about their assurance. Once she had been disposed of, Carrie realised, they would be moving into the next stage of open attacks on human populations.

They also possibly guessed that the Council was about to unleash the full might of the Unity upon them. The time for subterfuge was over. They were preparing for all-out war.

Held within the frame of the paperclip, Carrie entered the abandoned warehouse. It was almost entirely dark inside save for shafts of moonlight that shone through the vandalised windows. The mechanical army clanked, tapped and ground its way in behind her. Not a single placktoid had spoken to Carrie since they had agreed to allow her friends to leave.

She shivered and wondered where they were going next. Or would they do it there?

The paperclip floated farther inside the warehouse, heading for a lift at the end. It was an industrial type: large with metal doors and only two buttons, one arrow pointing up and the other pointing down.

By radio or some other kind of electronic communication, the placktoids activated the 'down' button. It lit up, and the lift doors opened. The wide, deep area within was dusty and dim. The paperclip carried her inside and several more placktoids followed. Their combined weight made the lift dip as they entered. Carrie thought about making a final appeal to the aliens but quickly dismissed the idea. She'd never before been able to persuade or trick a placktoid about anything. There was no reason to think she would be able to do it now. Especially now that they held all the cards.

The lift doors closed, and with a click and whirr, it began its descent. The doors were only on the outside of the lift. A wall of old bricks slid past as they went down into the basement. The lift arrived at a second set of doors and jerked as it halted. The doors opened and the placktoids left in reverse order, with Carrie and the paperclip exiting last. The sight that awaited her made her gasp.

In all her encounters with the mechanical aliens, Carrie had never seen many of them at a time. She'd mostly been dragged before the leader of whichever particular group she'd been dealing with. There had to be hundreds of thousands of them at a minimum, she knew. They had an entire planet to themselves after all. But she'd never imagined what that would look like in reality.

The placktoids had extended the warehouse basement so far and wide, Carrie couldn't make out the limits of the space. Its boundaries were lost in the darkness, and between her and those invisible far distant walls stood placktoids beyond count.

As her gaze roved the massive crowd that was awaiting her, she saw many new types of mechanical aliens. Some resembled the egg-shaped, undifferentiated kind that the present-day placktoids had evolved from. Others were entirely new forms, some of which seemed almost impossible. Among them were some products of her factory too—smaller kinds that she'd guessed were the new forms the placktoids had created of themselves. Organic and capable of sexual reproduction, these would be the placktoids that would lead the colonisation of defeated planets following their invasions.

Carrie's mind leapt unwillingly to the amount of destruction this number of placktoids could wreak on the people of Britain. No doubt this wasn't all of them either, she realised as she recalled the labyrinth of tunnels the placktoids had already dug throughout the U.K. She quailed at the thought of what lay in store for her country's people when she was gone.

The wait for what was to happen to her was becoming unbearable. She began to wish the aliens would just get it over with. But her torture continued. Another pathway opened, and Carrie's paperclip floated into it. The placktoids on each side remained still and silent as they passed, but the smaller products of Carrie Hatchett Enterprises moved around.

Their behaviour attracted Carrie's attention as she floated along. Their movements were sluggish or they jerked in a random, odd way. Carrie recalled her encounter with them at her company's factory in Northampton. Their behaviour then had been quite different. Once they'd given up pretending they were inanimate, they'd been full of aggressive, belligerent energy.

The paperclip flew on, deep into the midst of the serried ranks of placktoids. Carrie had no doubt that it was taking her to their leader. She wondered what it was. Before, she'd met commanding placktoids that looked like office shredders or 3D printers. She couldn't imagine what form the ultimate head of these multitudes of placktoids would take, except that it had to be a creature of deepest evil.

As they continued, the larger mechanical aliens grew fewer and the smaller devices increased in number. These new third-generation placktoids were also moving slowly. Some were lying on their sides, while others were dragging themselves along, often with one or more of their parts trailing.

Carrie pressed her hands against the invisible forcefield that held her, leaning forward to peer out at the products her company had made. What was wrong with them?

The paperclip halted and the forcefield evaporated, sending Carrie tumbling out, carried forward by her own weight. She hit the floor head first and sat up, rubbing her nose. "I really need to stop doing that."

The bare, dirt ground was ridged where a plackoid machine had carved out the space. It was also icy cold. Carrie clamped her hands under her armpits to try to warm them as she wondered where the placktoid leader was. Perhaps the aliens would make her wait there. The smaller devices ranged all around.

The aliens that had accompanied her and the paperclip in the lift had been left behind while Carrie's transportation had zoomed ahead. They were just beginning to catch up. The first of them arrived. It looked something like a hole punch and when it spoke its voice was high and piercing.

"We demand that you help our comrades."

Its communication caught her entirely off guard. Carrie had been expecting it to say something slightly different. Something like, 'Prepare to die,' or 'Your executioner approaches.' To give herself time to think up a suitable response, she stood and blew on her cupped hands. The best reply she could come up with, however, was, "What?"

"Do not try to deceive us, Carrie Hatchett," said the hole punch placktoid. "We know what you have done. We demand that you repair those of us you have damaged, or you will suffer a long and painful death. You must know how to repair them."

Carrie thought back over the time since she'd first been alerted to the placktoid invasion of Earth. She couldn't recall damaging any of them. In fact, many of them had damaged her. Probably several of the ones who now surrounded them. Yet, as her mind returned to the small devices which seemed to have something wrong with them, she began to make a connection. Not quite able to put her finger on it, she continued to stall. "I haven't hurt any of you."

"Cease lying," exclaimed the hole punch. "You know what you have done and you know the remedy. Only a genius among humans could so consistently thwart our plans." Carrie winced as its voice penetrated her ear drums.

From behind her came another voice: "Stop it."

Carrie turned. It was the paperclip who had carried

her there who had spoken.

"Your threats will get us nowhere," the paperclip continued. "We need Carrie Hatchett's help. Our people are suffering."

So there *was* something wrong with the devices. But what? Carrie's potential reprieve from imminent death appeared to evaporate. Her factory workers had merely followed the instructions they'd been given by Matthias Cowper, the original owner. The devices had been designed by dandrobians. She didn't know how to fix whatever problem it was they had, though now she had an explanation as to why the placktoids thought she was responsible. It was her company after all. But if she told the placktoids she couldn't help them, she could kiss her slim advantage goodbye.

She stamped her numb feet. "I'll help you," she said, "but first..." She stopped as another idea occurred to her. It would be wise to milk this situation for all it was worth.

"What?" asked the paperclip. "What is your request? If you can repair our broken citizens, we will give you whatever is within our power to bestow."

"Bring back the British Prime Minister from your planet immediately."

After a short pause, the placktoid said, "We will do it."

Familiar green specks instantly appeared in a narrow open space. The swirling mist that formed opened at its centre, and the PM arrived. Carrie went over to her. She was weak and sunburned, but she was alive. She needed prompt medical attention.

"Now will you help us?" the paperclip asked.

"Wait," Carrie replied. "Open another gateway and send this woman to the nearest hospital. You know what a hospital is, right? It's where humans go when they're sick or..." Carrie tried to think of a way to describe the concept of illness to these non-organic beings, "broken."

A second gateway opened. Carrie helped the barely conscious PM into it. She would have to trust the placktoids to send the poor woman to the right place.

With the Prime Minister saved, Carrie wondered what else she could make the placktoids do. The obvious request was that they would give up their plan to invade the galaxy and to leave Earth. But there was no way they would do that. That had been their ambition for as long as she'd known them, and perhaps for the millennia they had waited on Dandrobia. While she considered how she could turn the situation to her advantage, Carrie played for time.

"So, what's wrong with these creatures?" she asked. "How are they broken?"

"You know what is wrong with them," burst out the hole punch. "She lies. Now that we have done what she asked, she will not help us."

"You must know what is wrong with them, Carrie Hatchett," said the paperclip. "You are the cause of their problem. You have defeated us at every turn. Now you have attacked our new generation. You have no mercy."

"Huh?" Carrie said. The paperclip's meaning remained a mystery, but she needed to tread carefully. If the placktoids really believed she'd damaged the devices and was refusing to fix them, things would turn out badly. "I mean...can you explain *exactly* what their problem is? I promise I'll do what I can to help."

"You are playing a game with us," said the paperclip, "but we have no choice but to play along. Our comrades who were manufactured on this planet began to break down after they encountered you at the breeding site. You did something to them. They began to break, but the problem did not only affect the ones you contacted. It has spread to others who were not there. You have invented an evil mechanism that passes system failures from one of them to the next. Now, most of our new generation is affected. If you tell us the method of repair and how to prevent the spread, we will spare your life."

Carrie, who had been jigging about while the damp, cold atmosphere penetrated her inadequate clothing, abruptly stopped. The devices had begun to break down after she'd been attacked by them at the factory? The problem had spread to others who hadn't been there? The connection that had begun to form at the back of her mind finally closed. The answer hit her along with the realisation that she was no longer sneezing or coughing. Her nose had stopped running and her headache had gone. She had finally got over her cold.

The same couldn't be said for the devices she'd unwittingly infected that evening at the factory. As partly organic beings, they'd caught her virus. Then they'd passed it on to others. That was what was wrong with the third generation placktoids—they were suffering from the common cold.

And if she cured them, the paperclip had said she could live. Except that the cold virus had no cure.

CHAPTER TWENTY-SEVEN

Carrie had checked over more than forty of the sick devices, yet she remained no closer to an answer to her problem. The best doctor in the world couldn't cure the third generation placktoids of their colds, let alone her. She'd suffered for three or four long days with the dreadful virus. It was a real stinker, and she knew just how the devices must feel.

If she'd had the first idea how to cure her cold, she would have done it for herself. Goodness knew how many remedies she'd tried. None of them had worked more than a little, so she seriously doubted they would have an effect on placktoids, assuming she could even figure out how to deliver them.

How could she give a placktoid a hot lemon and honey drink? Where would she rub Vicks ointment or apply raw onion slices? How could a placktoid chew garlic?

The problem was beyond her, but she dared not tell

that to the mechanical aliens. The minute they knew she couldn't help them, it would be curtains for her.

From the impatient movements of the plactoids, Carrie could tell she didn't have much longer before one of them demanded some kind of answer from her. She wondered what they were saying to each other via electronic communication. Probably arguing about the method of her execution, she guessed. Her hope for escape from her fate seemed to have slipped from her grasp. Carrie comforted herself that she'd been able to save the Prime Minister.

As she turned the devices over, pretending to examine them, she looked back on her short life. She marvelled at how far she had come since her interview with Ms. Bass and unexpectedly landing the job as call centre supervisor. She'd also grown and learned a lot in her time as Transgalactic Intercultural Community Crisis Liaison Officer. It seemed odd that these strange items of equipment were partly responsible for her journey.

One thing she'd learned, and one thing she'd wanted to put right at Carrie Hatchett Enterprises, was that it was best to lay things on the line. She'd wanted to amend the original complaints manual so that customers were no longer given the runaround until they gave up on their complaint. She'd wanted to be frank and upfront with them about what her company could and couldn't do. Now that she was in a corner with the plactoids, she decided that honesty might be the best policy there too. It wasn't like she had another option. She had to tell them something, and in the circumstances, the truth was no worse than any subterfuge.

She returned to the waiting placktoids, stepping through their sick comrades dotted all around. "Look," she said, "I'm going to be frank with you. Your comrades have caught something called a virus. I didn't mean to give it to them. I didn't even know I could. It's because they're partly organic. Viruses infect us organic beings. They're all around us—in the air, on surfaces, in water—and some of them make us very sick, or 'broken' as you call it."

This time, Carrie had to wait several minutes for an answer. "We think we understand your meaning," the paperclip replied. "We also have these problems with our electronic systems, but we can remove the invader and isolate the affected machine to prevent the problem from spreading."

"Yes," said Carrie, "I think I know what you mean. That's a different kind of virus. We have those too. Maybe you can tell when that kind of virus infects you. The problem with viruses that affect organic life forms is that we can pass them on even before we know we've caught them—before we show any symptoms. So they spread around like wildfire and there's little we can do to stop them.

"The virus your new generation has is called a cold." She took a breath. "I'm sorry, but I can't cure them. We haven't developed a cure for the cold virus. I'd love to tell you something different, I really would. I'd love to walk out of here alive and free, but that's the truth of it."

"What?" shrieked the hole punch. "Our fellows can never be repaired? You have damaged thousands of our beloved comrades. You will regret your actions for the short, painful remainder of your life." The creature snapped and moved towards her.

"Wait," Carrie said, holding up her hands. "I haven't finished. The illness only lasts a few days. These devices will get better, if they react like humans. They'll repair themselves and eradicate the virus from their system. You don't need me to fix them."

"Even better," the hole punch said. "I am overjoyed that our next generation will overcome this setback without your help, though it was very foolish of you to tell us. We no longer need you. Prepare to die, Carrie Hatchett."

The machine edged closer. Carrie moved backwards. "You don't understand, though. The ones who were infected will get better, but they've already passed the cold on to others. The virus is in the population now. You'll never get rid of it. Every partly organic placktoid you create will catch it." An idea occurred to Carrie. Perhaps there was an escape route from the placktoid invasion after all.

"That's only one cold virus," she went on. "There are thousands of them. Tens of thousands, maybe. If these devices could catch my cold, they could catch any of them. And the cold is only one kind of virus. Organic life forms are infected by many more. Colds only make you feel ill for a few days, but other viruses are deadly. They can kill. Earth is rife with them. Your part-organic generation isn't prepared for that, is it?"

It was a guess, but Carrie was sure she was correct. The dandrobians had no doubt genetically engineered themselves to be impervious to viruses, probably so long ago they didn't even remember that viruses existed. They hadn't given the devices the same protection.

The hole punch halted. The placktoids were in furious, rapid, silent communication.

"If you don't believe me," she said, "check the data stored in our universities and hospitals. I'm sure you can do that. You've infiltrated all our other systems. You didn't bother checking medical information, did you? Or you might have guessed what was wrong with your comrades."

Still the placktoids were motionless and quiet. Carrie's heart was in her mouth. She hardly dared to hope that her words might be making a difference to the placktoids' invasion plan. She found she was no longer cold. Adrenaline had sent warmth into her fingertips and toes.

The mechanical aliens seemed to be teetering on the edge of a momentous decision. A tiny push could send them over the edge.

"If you want to save your new generation," Carrie said, "your only hope is to leave with them immediately. Before they catch another virus. The next one might not only last a few days. The next one could be fatal."

The idea that she could persuade the placktoids to abandon their invasion plans in order to protect their next evolutionary stage was insane. But she had nothing to lose. It was worth a try, and everything she had told the placktoids was absolutely true. They would know from the checking they were undoubtedly carrying out that she wasn't misleading them. The question was, did they care enough for their third generation to move them off Earth and isolate them from other organic life forms? And if they did, would they still continue their invasion plan with that part of it missing?

As if in answer to her musings, the green dust of a gateway flickered into life not far from where she was standing. Carrie stepped to one side as the specks increased and began to swirl. She wondered if the portal was intended for her or the devices.

All around, placktoids were finally stirring after their prolonged period of stillness. The entire massive space seemed to be in motion as the thousands of placktoids shifted and came clacking, clinking and clanking to life. The air soon filled with the sounds of machinery moving. Carrie put her hands over her ears as the sound redoubled, echoing from the ceiling.

None of the placktoids felt like informing her about what was happening. They began to pick up the sick devices and carry them towards the spinning portal. The first placktoid disappeared through it. They were leaving. Or some of them were. Could they all be departing? Carrie could hardly believe it. There had to be a catch somewhere. Maybe they were only taking the devices away until they got better, or maybe they wouldn't use them but would continue the invasion.

Her first thought was to try to sneak away, but as the only human in the crowd, her plan was hopeless. Carrie noticed the paperclip who had brought her to the hideout was hovering nearby as if supervising the exodus. She went over to it, hoping it would deign to provide her with some answers.

She touched its frame. The metal was cold and thrumming with an oscillating vibration. "Please," she said, "What's happening? Are you going?"

"We are returning to our planet," the paperclip replied. "Once again, Carrie Hatchett, you have won. But this time is different. Before, we wished to continue in our quest to assume our rightful place as galactic leaders over you inferior organic life forms. Now, we forsake and reject that ambition.

"But we made a terrible mistake in mixing our kind with yours and creating these weak, vulnerable hybrids. We had hoped to hone our development with the aid of sexual reproduction, subject to selective pressures that would ensure the survival of placktoids best fitted to whatever environment we encountered. But our experience on Earth has made us understand that organic life is far from ideal. We checked Earth's information about viruses and discovered that you had told us the truth. Organic life forms suffer from diseases that are sometimes horrible and incurable.

"We are no longer interested in leading the organic species of the galaxy. We had a dream of the excellence we could achieve once we were in power, but now that dream is gone. You disgust us. We do not wish to associate with your kind any longer. We will retreat to our world, tend to our poor hybrids, and create our own utopia there, uncontaminated by organic life."

"You..." Carrie gasped, "you're leaving? Forever?"

"We have no reason to stay. As we speak, placktoids across your world are departing. They are returning to our beautiful planet, where we will create our own, disease-free paradise."

CHAPTER TWENTY-EIGHT

The doorbell at the London flat rang. Dave's heart rose, but only for a moment. The person at the door couldn't possibly be Carrie. Rogue ran barking down the hall in reaction to the sound and Toodles followed more sedately, her tail up and her gait sprightly. Dave walked slowly after them. It was going to be hard to look after Carrie's pets while they gradually realised their mistress was never coming back.

Dave turned the latch and eased the door open—he had fixed it enough to be able to close and lock it but he'd put in no more effort than that. There was no point as he would be leaving the next day. Holding the edge of the door tight to the hinges, he peered around it. Belinda was waiting outside.

He opened the door wider. "Hi. Come in."

Belinda gave him a sympathetic look as she stepped into the hall. "I heard about Carrie. Thought I'd come around and offer my condolences."

Dave nodded and motioned to the living room. "Would you like some tea?"

"That would be lovely, thanks."

"I've got another visitor," Dave said. "But I'll let you two introduce yourselves. She knows all about the Transgalactic Council and everything, so you don't need to worry about giving anything away."

"Oh, okay."

While Belinda and the actor, whose name was Jodie, got acquainted, Dave remained in the kitchen making the tea. He had already set the furniture to rights and cleaned up a little so the place was presentable. He would leave it to Jodie to fill Belinda in on what had happened when Carrie left with the placktoids. He didn't feel much like talking.

As he was looking out the kitchen window into the darkness, a paw touched his thigh. Rogue was sitting at his feet, looking up at him expectantly. Dave patted the dog's head. "I wish I could help you, mate, but I can't. I can't bring her back."

Rogue tilted his head as if trying to understand Dave's words. He pawed Dave's thigh again.

"How about a treat?" Dave asked. He went to the cupboard. It was bare except for the cat and dog food Carrie had bought. He took down a packet of Premium Grillers Natural Dog Snacks and held it out to the dog. "Want a treat?"

Rogue sniffed at the packet but didn't seem interested in its contents. Dave took out a snack and threw it on the floor. Rogue sniffed it but didn't eat it.

He pawed Dave's thigh for a third time.

"Walk?" Dave asked. "Do you want to go walkies?"

Rogue's tail wagged a little, but then he lay down on his stomach and rested his head on his paws. His eyes drooped sadly.

Dave sighed. He poured the boiled water into mugs with tea bags and carried them out to the living room. Belinda and Jodie were chatting away as he went in, getting along like a house on fire.

"Actually," Belinda was saying, "I'm half-dandrobian myself, believe it or not. After recent events, I feel compelled to add that it isn't my favourite half. I feel like I should apologise on behalf of my relatives. I'm so sorry for what they did to you."

"Don't worry about it," Jodie replied. "It isn't like you locked me up yourself, is it? Besides, after everything I've learned tonight, I'm almost glad they kidnapped me. I can hardly believe it. It's like a script for an episode of my series. Aliens? Sentient killer robots? Oh, what am I saying?" She gently touched Dave's arm as he placed the tray on the coffee table. "That was incredibly insensitive of me. I'm so sorry."

He smiled tightly. "It's fine. Really." He sat down. "Help yourselves to tea."

"Poor Carrie," said Jodie.

"Yes," Belinda said. "Poor Carrie."

The silence that followed was awkward, but Dave was in no mood to think up something to say. He was beyond exhausted and he didn't know how he was ever going to come to terms with what had happened that night.

"Errruorerrrrrhch was telling me you're leaving Earth in the morning, Dave," Belinda said.

"Yeah, I am. The Council decided, in view of Carrie's service, to let me take her pets off-planet. I'll look for a boring, out-of-the-way place the placktoids won't be interested in for a while. Errruorerrrrrh will help me find somewhere they'll be safe, hopefully for the rest of their lives."

"Do you think the war's going to last that long?" Jodie asked.

Belinda nodded and her expression turned grave. "The Unity will be here any minute," she said to Dave. "That's what Errruorerrrrrhch told me anyway. I'm surprised none of our astronomers have spotted them yet."

Rogue barked and bounded from the kitchen down the hall to the front door. Dave could hear his claws scratching at it. The small ginger form of Toodles also trotted past the open living room doorway. Miaows joined Rogue's frantic barking.

"What's wrong with them, I wonder?" Dave asked. "I hope they don't wake the neighbours up."

"Is there someone at the door?" asked Jodie.

"I don't think so," Dave replied. "I didn't hear the bell ring."

"This is a bit of a rough area," Belinda said. "I would be careful about opening the door this time of night."

Dave went to the living room window to look through the curtains. "Jodie, could you turn off the light? I can't see outside."

When the living room light wasn't reflecting on the window, Dave could see the shadowy area outside the flat. It was hard to view the space on the other side of the front door from the angle, but he could make out a figure standing there. The person was quite short and was leaning their head against the door.

Dave cursed, using a word he rarely said, and flew through the living room. He ripped open the front door, breaking all his repairs.

"Carrie!"

She fell into his arms.

* * *

Dave brought his friend into the living room.

"Oh my goodness," Jodie exclaimed at the sight of them and jumped up from the sofa.

Dave sat Carrie down and held her hands. They were freezing. She was pale and cold and seemed only half conscious.

"Belinda," Dave said. "Get a duvet from one of the bedrooms. Carrie, drink this." He held up a mug of warm, sweet tea to her lips. She sipped it, grimaced, swallowed, and sipped some more. The hot liquid seemed to revive her.

Rogue was bouncing on and off the sofa, running in circles and barking loudly. Thumping sounds came through the ceiling from the neighbours, voicing their complaint. Belinda arrived with a duvet, which she wrapped around Carrie's shoulders. Toodles immediately climbed onto her mistress' lap and under the covering.

"Should I phone for an ambulance?" Jodie asked.

"Yes," Dave said.

"No," said Carrie. "I'm okay. I'm just tired. I walked a long way, and it's so cold outside. I'll feel better soon." She drank some more tea. The colour began to return to her cheeks. "Dave."

"What?"

"I've got a confession to make."

"Huh?"

"I really don't like your tea."

He made a noise somewhere between a laugh and a sob. Taking his friend's hands, he rubbed them between his own. "Are you sure you're going to be all right?"

Carrie nodded. "I am. We all are. The placktoids have gone."

"What?" exclaimed Dave, Belinda and Jodie.

As Carrie told her story, Belinda called Errruorerrrrrhch on her communication device so that she could listen in. Rogue slowly settled down. He eventually came to rest with his head on Carrie's foot, where he quickly fell asleep.

After Carrie had told them about watching the placktoids departing through the gateway, Dave asked, "Did you stay to watch the last of them go?"

She shook her head. "I'd still be there now if I had. But they're all going. I'm certain of it. And that's super lucky for us. The Council gateways could never stay open so long as theirs did. If the placktoids' or dandrobians' gateway technology can do that, they could have the galaxy at their mercy."

"So we're lucky we're disease-ridden, virus-transmitting, organic life forms?" Jodie asked.

"Yeah," said Carrie.

"So if you didn't stick around," said Dave, "what did you do?"

"I left of course. I took the lift up to ground level, and I went out of the warehouse. None of them tried to stop me. After that, I walked here."

"You walked here from where?" Dave asked.

"Canary Wharf."

"Canary Wharf? That's miles," he exclaimed.

"Tell me about it," Carrie replied. "But I didn't have a choice. No phone, no money, no cards. I got lost three times too." She bent over to untie her bootlaces. "Do you mind if I lie down?"

"Give me a minute and I'll make up your bed," Dave said.

Carrie yawned. "Thanks, but I'd rather sleep here." She threw a couple of cushions to one end of the sofa, pulled up her legs and stretched herself out. As she adjusted the duvet, Toodles could be seen moving to a new position next to Carrie's stomach. Rogue didn't stir.

Jodie stood up. "Time for me to go home and let you both get some rest. What a day this has been."

Errruorerrrrrhch's voice came through Belinda's communicator: "Transgalactic Intercultural...Carrie, you have done an excellent job. We are suspending Unity movements while we confirm that the placktoid threat has passed. The escaped dandrobians will be apprehended and returned to their home planet at the earliest opportunity. Dave and Belinda, I expect you to begin work on this task when you are sufficiently rested."

"Yes, we will," Belinda said.

Dave gathered the mugs of tea onto the tray, ready to take out to the kitchen. He would have to fix the door again before he could go to bed. He'd quickly propped it closed while Carrie was telling her story, but the winter's chill had penetrated the flat, though Carrie looked cosy and warm underneath the duvet.

"If that's all, Errruorerrrrrhch," said Belinda, "I'll be leaving now too. Plenty to do in the morning."

"Yes, that is everything I wish to say to you at this time," Errruorerrrrrhch replied. "Except, I would like to reiterate my earlier commendation. Carrie Hatchett, we at the Council greatly appreciate your exemplary service. We hope that you will long continue in your role as Transgalactic Intercultural Community Crisis Liaison Officer."

"Sorry, Errruorerrrrrh," Dave said. "She's asleep."

Thanks for reading!

Reviews are very important to the success of a book. If you enjoyed *Mission Improbable*, please consider leaving a review. Even a few sentences help.

Sign up to my reader group for a free copy of *Carrie Hatchett's Christmas*, the standalone novelette in the Carrie Hatchett, Space Adventurer series, and for exclusive notice of new releases, advanced reader opportunities and other interesting stuff:

http://jjgreenauthor.com/

(I won't send spam or pass on your details to a third party.)

Scroll ahead for a sneak preview of Carrie Hatchett's Christmas.

ALSO BY J.J. GREEN

STAR MAGE SAGA

SPACE COLONY ONE SERIES

SHADOWS OF THE VOID SERIES

LOST TO TOMORROW

THERE COMES A TIME
A SCIENCE FICTION COLLECTION

DAWN FALCON
A FANTASY COLLECTION

CARRIE HATCHETT'S CHRISTMAS

CHAPTER ONE - SANTA'S GROTTO

Ms. Emily Wainwright stood holding the hand of a little girl in a queue that snaked from the entrance of Selfridges and down Oxford Street, London. Snow had begun to fall, the first that season, and though it was only four in the afternoon, the street lights began to wink on, supplementing the rainbow hues of Christmas lights, bright in the approaching late afternoon dusk. The child shivered a little. Emily looked down and smiled and held her hand tighter.

The little girl wasn't her daughter. Ms. Wainwright worked in a children's home, and the child lived at the home, the most recent of a long string of residences she had lived in since she was born. In Emily's experience, the girl's history was familiar. Babies, especially foundling babies such as the girl had been, were usually easy to place with loving adoptive parents, providing they fitted within the spectrum of what society considered normal. Sadly, the little girl's appearance didn't fall in that category, and no one returned to see her after their first visit.

Emily Wainwright had a big heart, but for some reason she'd never found anyone to share it with, and she'd formed an attachment to the child that she knew was unprofessional. Little Beth Lam wouldn't have been a burden to her. Named after Lambeth, the London borough in which she'd been found as a newborn, she was a pleasure to be around, and though no doctor had been able to diagnose the cause of her physical oddities, all had concluded that she was otherwise normal in every way. Except that for the last few months Beth had failed to gain any weight, and each day grew paler and more tired.

"Will I see Santa soon?" asked the child, turning her peculiar eyes up at her guardian.

"Yes, Beth," replied Emily, "not much longer now. We're near the doors, and when we get inside we'll be warmer."

"I'm so excited," said Beth, jumping on the tips of her toes.

The temperature was falling as fast as the snow, now that the winter sun had set, but, as was typical for the child, she didn't complain. Emily's own hands were numb, and with her small frame, the little girl must have been chilled. She wore the cheap secondhand clothes all the looked-after children wore. The hood of her thin parka was pulled down over her head to keep her warm as well as hide her deformities from the gaze of curious Christmas shoppers.

A group of carollers were singing to the accompaniment of handbells to entertain the waiting customers. People towards the front of the queue began to move through Selfridges' wide doorway and into the department store. Those waiting ahead of the woman and child closed the gap and the pair followed, until at last they were inside and basking in the cranked-up heat of oil-fed furnaces.

Beth gasped aloud, causing the family waiting in front to turn around. A boy stared at her, saying, "Urghh...what's wrong with that girl, Mummy?" His mother tugged on his hand, turning him to face forward. "Don't be rude," she hissed.

A shadow of pain flickered over Beth's face, but the little girl had grown used to taunts and comments, and she had learned to ignore them. "It's beautiful," she said, referring to Santa's Grotto, which occupied a full third of Selfridge's ground floor.

Indeed it was beautiful. Even Emily, who had been coming to Santa's Grotto at Selfridges for as long as she could remember, was impressed. Her mother had brought her every Christmas when she was growing up, until she was really much too big. Later, she had brought nephews, nieces and now looked-after children who often had no parents to bring them. But in all those Christmases she had never seen a display more magical.

Rocky walls stretched from floor to ceiling, their realistic crags dusted with snow that looked freshly fallen, sparkling faintly in the shop's blazing overhead lights. A path wove from Selfridges' front door to the secretive entrance to the grotto, bordered by holly, mistletoe, ivy and pine that scented the air with a resinous odour. Animal figures appeared to gambol through the green growth: foxes, hares, weasels in their winter coats; and birds perched in the branches: snowy owls, red-breasted robins, and speckled thrushes. All seemed to have frozen to stillness only a second earlier. Blue-white snow encrusted the path and forest scene, and Emily and Beth crunched it with their footsteps as they followed the diminishing queue slowly disappearing through the grotto entrance.

"Will I sit on Santa's lap?" asked Beth.

"Of course you will."

"And can I ask for a present? Whatever I want?"

Emily's heart ached. She knew too well what gift most of the looked-after children asked Santa for: something even he wasn't able to provide.

"You can ask for whatever you want," replied Emily, "but Santa might not be able to give it to you."

"Not even if I've been very good?"

"Not even if you've been very, very good, Beth." Emily turned her head to one side and ran a finger under an eye before turning back to the girl wearing a bright smile. "But he'll give you a present, and would you like a mince pie to eat on the way home?"

"Oh, yes please," exclaimed the child.

Another set of people entered the grotto, and the queue shuffled forward several steps. Emily and Beth were among the trees now. They were hung with gorgeous baubles, shining in iridescent hues. Beth pulled on Emily's hand as she leaned close to gaze at her reflection in a shiny surface.

A cry came from with the grotto. It was a deep voice, a man's voice, shouting in alarm. The hum of conversation in the queue abruptly stopped, and the people looked around as if to check that others had heard the same thing. Another cry, louder, sounded, followed by the shouts of more voices. Looks of puzzlement in the queue turned to alarm, and some members edged away from the grotto entrance.

"Ms. Wainwright," said Beth, looking up at her guardian for reassurance. "What was that?"

But Emily had no reassurance to give. "Perhaps we'd better come back tomo—"

A bang shook the grotto, vibrating the floor beneath Emily and Beth's feet. The queue melted and people began to run for the doors. The rest of Selfridges' customers also began rapidly leaving. Emily scooped Beth up into her arms and tried to fight her way through the stampede, struggling to keep her feet.

"Please," she gasped as a large man pushed roughly past, almost causing her to drop the child. Woman and girl were carried through Selfridges' doors and into the street, where Emily had no choice but to follow in the direction of the crowd as she was swept along. At a Tube entrance, however, she took her chance to escape. She stepped to one side out of the flow of the throng into the lee of the Underground entry wall.

213

Setting Beth on her feet, Emily peered out from their place of safety and back towards Selfridges. She'd heard nothing but the noise of the crowd since the bang. Shoppers continued to flood from the department store's doors, but no smoke or fire was to be seen, and no one seemed injured. Sirens wailed up Oxford Street, and in the distance the lights of emergency service vehicles flashed.

Wary of stepping out into the mad rush with a small child, Emily waited a few more moments, watching the crowd and hoping for a gap in the foot traffic, and this was how she got such a good view of the cause of the disturbance, though she didn't know it at the time.

The first thing she saw of them were the points of their green felt hats, low down among the shoulders of the escaping shoppers. A sparkling scarlet feather waved to the side of each green point as the elves approached. The frontrunner confirmed Emily's suspicion that the hats belonged to Santa's elves. He—it appeared to be a he, though Emily found it hard to be sure, as the elves looked quite androgynous—he was wearing a bright green tunic that matched his hat, bright green leggings, a silver belt and pointed silver boots. The rest of the elves appeared behind their leader, dodging and weaving through Selfridge's advancing customers like long-distance runners making their way to the front of a race.

Emily had only a few seconds' close-up view of the faces of Santa's short, plump helpers as they passed by, but what she saw made her gasp.

CARRIE HATCHETT'S CHRISTMAS

ABOUT THE AUTHOR

J.J. Green was born in London's East End within the sound of the church bells of St. Mary Le Bow, Cheapside, which makes her a bona fide Cockney. She first left the U.K. as a young adult and has lived in Australia and Laos. She currently lives in Taipei, Taiwan, where she entertains the locals with her efforts to learn Mandarin. Writers she admires include Philip K. Dick, Ursula Le Guin, Douglas Adams, Connie Willis and Ann Leckie.

Green writes science fiction, fantasy, weird, dark and humorous tales, and her work has appeared in Lamplight, Perihelion, Saturday Night Reader and other magazines and websites. Sign up to her mailing list at http://eepurl.com/bj4v4z and follow her on Facebook https://www.facebook.com/JJGreenAuthor/ and Twitter https://twitter.com/Infinitebook1

15575372R00130

Printed in Germany
by Amazon
Distribution